"Lord Cromis, you are here to hunt."

Indeed he was. He inclined his head.

"Do not. The *baan* has brought doom to many, and will make no exception of yourself. Plainly we have one of the Eight Beasts among us. Since it has chosen Duirinish for this incarnation, Duirinish must bear the brunt. I have no desire to see you brought maimed and destroyed from the Marshes, sir...Let someone else dispose of it."

"Had a man said that to me, I would have spat at his feet. Lady, I am of the Sixth House; for a hundred generations the Beast has felled an ancestor of mine. It may be my fate to destroy it once and for all..."

VIRICONIUM NIGHTS

M. JOHN HARRISON

ACE FANTASY BOOKS
NEW YORK

Acknowledgments

"The Lamia and Lord Cromis" originally appeared in *New Worlds
Quarterly 1*, Sphere Books (London), © 1971 by the author.

"Lamia Mutable" originally appeared in *Again,
Dangerous Visions*, edited by Harlan Ellison, Doubleday & Co.
(New York), © 1972 by the author.

"Viriconium Knights" originally appeared in
Elsewhere, edited by Terri Windling and Mark Alan Arnold, Ace Books
(New York), © 1981 by the author.

"Events Witnessed From a City" originally appeared in *The Machine in
Shaft Ten*, Panther (London), © 1975 by the author.

"The Lords of Misrule" originally appeared in *Savoy Dreams*
(Manchester), © 1983 by the author.

"Strange Great Sins" originally appeared in *Interzone 5*
(London), © 1983 by the author.

VIRICONIUM NIGHTS

An Ace Fantasy Book / published by arrangement with
the author

PRINTING HISTORY
Ace Original / August 1984

ISBN: 0-441-86570-4

Ace Fantasy Books are published by The Berkley Publishing Group,
200 Madison Avenue, New York, New York 10016.
PRINTED IN THE UNITED STATES OF AMERICA

To Algis Budrys,
one of the true-mouthed lads.

Table of Contents

Author's Note

In the Viriconium stories I have favored increasingly a thematic rather than a chronological unity.

Viriconium was never intended to be the same place twice. New kings come and go, new philosophies spring up overnight. The very streets shift from story to story. All that remains, as the earth grows older and the fabric of reality forgets what it is supposed to be, is a whisper of continuity: place names which seem familiar; characters we seem to have heard of before; the imperfect repetition of this or that significant event. Even the name of the city changes. The world is a muddled old woman, obsessed with the futility of action in the face of contingency and an absurd universe. What seemed clear to her yesterday she remembers today only by remaking it. . . .

Thus the city presented here might as easily be a precursor as a relic of the one described in *The Pastel City, A Storm of Wings,* or *In Viriconium.*

The Lamia and Lord Cromis

1

LORD TEGEUS-CROMIS, sometime soldier and sophisticate of Viriconium, the Pastel City, who imagined himself to be a better poet than swordsman, sat at evening in the long, smoky parlor of the Blue Metal Discovery, chief inn of Duirinish. Those among his fellow-customers who knew something of traveling—and there were not too many of them—regarded him with a certain respect, for it was rumored that he had lately arrived from the capital, coming by the high paths through Monar, to Mam Sodhail and The High Leedale, which was no mean achievement. Winter comes early to the hills about Duirinish, and hard.

They watched him circumspectly. For himself, tegeus-Cromis found no similar interest in them, but sat with a jug of wine by his slim white left hand, listening to the north wind drive sleet across the bleak cobbles of Replica Square and against the bottle-glass windows of the inn.

He was a tall man, thin and cadaverous. He had slept little during his journey, and his green eyes were tired in the dark hollows above his high and prominent cheekbones.

He wore a heavy cloak of bice velvet; a tabard of antique leather set with iridium studs; tight mazarine velvet breeches; and calf-length boots of pale blue suede. The hand that curled around the jug of wine was weighted, according to the custom of the time, with bulky rings of nonferrous metals intagliated with involved ciphers and sphenograms. Beneath his cloak, the other rested on the pommel of his plain long-sword, which, contrary to the custom of the times, had no name.

Occupied by his wine and by consideration of the purpose which had brought him there at such a cold time, he was not disposed to talk: a circumstance the local clientele—in the main, fat merchants of the fur-and-metal trade, nouveau riche and pretentious—were loath to accept. They had twice invited him to sit with them around the massive roaring fireplace, eager to capture even so minor a lord. But he preferred to huddle in his cloak on the periphery of the room, in shadow. They left him to himself after the second refusal, whispering that the evening was chilly enough without his morose, ascetic features and his cold courtesy.

He was amused by their reaction. He ate a light meal, and afterward took a measure of good cocaine from a small box of chased pewter, sniffing it carefully up, his smile faint and withdrawn. Evening wore into night, and he did not move. He was waiting for someone, but not for the woman in the hooded purple cloak who came in accompanied only by a gust of wind and a flurry of sleet, at midnight.

He raised his heavy eyelids and watched her in.

She threw back her hood; her hair spilled down; long and roan, it blew about her delicate triangular face in the draft from the closing door. Her eyes were violet, flecked with colors he found difficult to name, depthless. There were no rings on her fingers, and her cloak was fastened by a copper clasp of complex design.

It was plain that the merchants knew her, but their welcome was stiff, a concerted multiplication of double chins, a brief collective nod; and for a moment a slight but discernible sense of embarrassment hung in the hot thick air about the fire. She paid them little notice, and they seemed thankful. Her cloak whispered past them, and she whispered to the innkeeper who, red-faced and perspiring, had thrust his flabby shoulders through the hatch that connected the parlor to his devils' kitchen.

When this exchange was done, and the serving hatch closed, she turned her attention to Cromis, slumped and still smiling faintly in his splendid cloak.

It was a strange look she gave him. In her queer eyes: habitual curiosity and blank indifference both, conflicting—as if she had lived many lives and metempsychoses under the Name Stars, seen the universal cycle through and again, but continued wearily about the surface of the world, waiting to be surprised by something. It was a strange look. Cromis met it openly, and was puzzled.

She came over to his table.

"Lady," he said, "I would stand, but—"

He indicated his little snuffbox, open on the tabletop. He saw that the clasp of her cloak was formed to represent mating dragonflies, or perhaps a complicated religious operating-symbol for ecstasy.

She nodded and smiled, her eyes unchanging.

"You are Lord tegeus-Cromis," she said. Her voice was unexpected, a rough, vibrant burr, an accent he could not place.

He raised his eyebrows. "The landlord?" he asked. She did not answer. "You flatter me by your attention," he said.

He poured her some wine.

"You had a scant reception from our good traders."

She took the cup and drank.

"All have made bids," she said, "as in their nature—to regard people as bales of fur, or ingots. (How do you regard people, lord?) Each has no wish that his friends discover that his bids were too low. Each therefore avoids me when in company of the others."

Cromis laughed. The merchants pricked up their ears.

But since she did not laugh with him but repeated the question he did not wish to answer, he changed the subject.

Later, he found that a great length of time had passed most pleasantly. He was puzzled with her yet, and wondered why she had picked him out. But he loved such company and loathed discourtesy, so he did not question her directly. The fire had died, the merchants had returned to their houses, the taverner hovered behind his hatch, amiable and yawning.

Suddenly she said to him:

"Lord Cromis, you are here to hunt."

And, indeed, he was. He inclined his head.

"Do not."

"But, lady—"

"The *baan* has brought doom to many, and will make no exception of yourself. Plainly, we have one of the Eight Beasts among us. Since it has chosen Duirinish for this incarnation, Duirinish must bear the brunt.

"I have no desire to see you brought maimed and destroyed from the Marshes, sir. . . ."

At this, he showed his teeth, and fondled the hilt of the nameless sword, and laughed loudly enough to disturb the innkeeper's light sleep.

"My lord," she said. "If I presume . . . ?"

He shook his head.

"Please, that was churlish of me. Your anxiety—let me dispel it—two companions hunt with me. Of one"—here he said a name—"you will have heard. I thought so. We will lay your Beast."

And, remembering the personal fate he might or might not be heir to:

"Besides, there are reasons as to why I should meet this *baan* if it is the one I suppose it to be."

He stood up. He was much taken with her and her mysterious concern. He said with the grave politeness of his times:

"Lady, I have a comfortable room above. It is late. Should you so wish, we could go there." And, having taken her arm, he asked, "Perhaps you would tell me your name?"

In the morning, he woke to an altercation in the yard below his window, and found her gone from his bed. Smoothing back the heavy graying hair that had escaped its suede fillet while he slept, he crossed the chilly oak floor and opened the shutters. A pale postdawn light filtered into the room, softening for a brief time his features, which remained bleak despite the pleasures of the night.

Down in the yard, the unpredictable weather of early winter had abandoned sleet and now offered frost instead, riming it thick on the cobbles and the half-doors of the stables, stiffening their hinges, bleaching the breath of the horses. The air had a metallic smell, a faint bitter taste, a thin echo of the stink of the Marsh.

Several shouting, gesticulating figures were gathered about two tired, laden packhorses and a fine blood mare almost nineteen hands high. Cromis could gain no clue as to the precise nature of the males, but the mare was plunging, striking out, and he saw that two of the figures were clad in the bright, clashing colors of fashionable Viriconium.

He closed the shutters gently, nodding to himself. Ignoring the subtle invitation of the pewter snuffbox—his habitual ennui having given way to a suppressed elation—he dressed quickly. He had this mannerism: as he went quietly down to the parlor to meet his visitors, his left hand strayed out unknown to him and caressed the black hilt of the sword that had been his doomed father's.

But his hands were still when Dissolution Kahn and Rotgob the dwarf, a mismatched enough couple, presented themselves at the parlor door, arguing over the stabling fees.

"But we *agreed* to share the expenses...." This in a powerful but injured tone.

"Ha. I was drunk. And besides"—with a reedy snigger—"I am a liar as well as a dwarf."

The Kahn was a massive man, heavy in the shoulder and heavier in the hip, with long sparse yellow hair that curled anarchically about his jowled and bearded features. His astonishing orange breeches were tucked into oxblood boots, his violet shirt had slashed and scalloped sleeves. A floppy-brimmed hat of dark brown felt, too small for his head, gave his face a sly and rustic caste.

"Every wench in the city knows *that*," he said with dignity. "Oh, hello, Cromis. You see: I found the little brute and brought him."

Rotgob, leaning on the doorpost beside the giant, greasy brown hair framing a blemished, ratlike face, was clad all in scarlet, his padded doublet amplifying the disproportion of barrel chest and twisted, skinny legs. He sniggered. His teeth were revolting.

"Who found who, stupid? Who bailed you out, eh? Pig!" Limping grotesquely, he scuttled over to Cromis's breakfast table. "I did!" He ate a bread roll. "It was a molestation charge again, Cromis. Next time they'll have his knackers off. We came as soon as we could." He rapped the table and did a little gleeful dance.

Cromis felt his lips break into a smile. "Sit down and eat, please do," he invited, wishing he might overcome his nature and greet his curious friends with less reserve.

"It is discovered, then?" asked the dwarf after they had finished, picking crumbs out of his mustache.

Cromis shook his head. "But I have heard rumors that it is one of the Eight. It has struck five times, up near Alves in the center of the city. They are much afraid of it here. I hope that it is the one I seek."

"They are cowards, merchants," said Dissolution Kahn.

"They are ordinary people, and cannot be held culpable for their fear—"

"Or anything else," interrupted the dwarf. He giggled.

"—You will feel fear before we are finished, Kahn. You know that."

"Aye, perhaps. If it is that one, I may—"

"The Sixth Beast of Viriconium," mused Rotgob. "Oh, you'll wet your drawers all right." Then: "It will be lairing in the Marsh. When do we start?"

"We must wait until it strikes again. I will have it put about that I am of the Sixth House, and then they will call me immediately." He laughed. "They will be glad to."

From a grossly ornamental sheath, Rotgob took a thing halfway between an extremely long stiletto and a rather short rapier and, leering, began to whet it. It was as famous as his name and his unlovable profession.

"Then, one more poor sod must die before we take the animal. That's a pity."

Looking at the little assassin, Cromis reflected that although gentler creatures lived, they had, on the whole, less character.

"I hope they're taking decent care of my mare," said Kahn. "She's a bit of a handful." A draft blew the smell of the Marsh strongly about the room. "No stink nastier," he observed, "and it upsets her."

2

Lord tegeus-Cromis spent the days that followed with the woman in the purple cloak, and he came to know her no better.

Once, they walked the spiral ascending streets near Alves and stood on the walls of the city to catch glimpses through the rain of the Marsh in the east and the sea in the west; up there she asked him why he wished so much to die, but, not having admitted it to himself before that moment, he could give no answer.

Once, he told her the following poem, which he had

composed in the Great Rust Desert during winter, chanting it to the accompaniment of a peculiar eastern instrument in a darkened room:

> Rust in our eyes . . . metallic perspectives trammel us in the rare earth north. . . . We are nothing but eroded men . . . wind clothing our eyes with white ice. . . . We are the swarf-eaters . . . hardened by our addiction, tasting acids. . . . Little to dream here, our fantasies are iron and icy echoes of bone. . . . Rust in our eyes, we who had once soft faces.

Once, she said to him, "The *baan* will kill you. Let someone else dispose of it." And he replied, "Had a man said that to me, I would have spat at his feet. Lady, as you know perfectly well, I am one of the Sixth House; the Sixth Beast destroyed my father, and he brought down the Beast; for a hundred generations and a hundred of its incarnations, the Beast has felled an ancestor of mine and died in doing so.

"It may be my fate to destroy it once and for all, by surviving the encounter. Lady, that is a matter of chance; but should the *baan* of Duirinish be that Beast, my duty is not."

Once, he came to understand the expression in her queer eyes, but when the dawn came he found that he had forgotten the revelation.

And the night before they called him to see a dead man in a dull house on a quiet cobbled street by Alves, she begged him to leave the city lest the *baan* be the doom of them both—a plea that he quite failed to understand.

In a chamber at the top of the house—

A place of midnight-blue silk drapes and small polished stone tables. There was a carpet like fine thick cellar mold, with an unwelcome stain. One stone wall had no hangings: to it were pinned charts of the night sky, done in a finicky hand. Beneath an open skylight, which framed the fading Name Stars and admitted almost reluctantly a clammy dawn—the corpse.

It had tumbled over a collection of astronomical instruments and lay clumsily among them, taking serene, empty-eyed measurement of a beautiful, complicated little orrery.

Cromis, like a crow in his black traveling cloak, noted the heavy fur robe of the dead astronomer, the fat, beringed fingers, and the fatter face; the graying flesh with its consistency of coarse blotting paper; the messy ringlets that covered what remained of the skull.

Even in death, the merchant had a faint air of embarrassment about him, as if he still sat by the fire in the Blue Metal Discovery on a sleety night, avoiding the eyes of the woman in the hooded purple cloak.

He would suffer no further embarrassment, for the top of his head had been torn raggedly off. Schooled in the signs, and having no need of a closer look, Cromis of the Sixth House knew that the ruined head was as empty as a breakfast egg, the painstaking mercenary brain—stolen?

He took up the orrery and absently turned the clockwork that set it in motion; jeweled planets hurried whirring round the splendid sun. Unconscious of the impression he had made on the third occupant of the room, he asked:

"Was nothing seen?"

Eyeing warily the lord who played so callously with a dead man's toys, the young uncomfortable proctor who had discovered the outrage shuddered and shook his head.

"No, my lord"—his eyes ranging the chamber, avoiding at all costs the corpse—"but a great noise woke some neighbors." He could not control his hands or his tremors.

"You have alerted the gatewardens?"

"Sir, they have seen nothing pass. But—"

"Yes?" impatiently.

"A fresh trail leads from the city, of blood. Sir?"

"Good."

"Sir? Sir, I am going to be sick."

"Then, leave."

The youth obeyed, and gazing over his shoulder at the grim corpse and grimmer avenger, stumbled through the door with the expression of a rabbit confronted by two ferrets. Cromis followed the motion of the planets through a complete cycle.

A commotion on the stairs.

"What a mess out there," said Rotgob the dwarf, bursting in and strutting round the stiff while Dissolution Kahn studied in puzzlement the star charts. "That is a very unprofessional job. Somebody is far too caught up with his own definition of death. Too much emotion to be art."

"You and the Kahn had better make ready our horses."

In the trembling light after dawn, they left the Stony City and rode into the north, following a clear spoor.

Rivermist rose fading toward the bleak sky in slender spires and pillars, hung over the slow water like a shroud. Duirinish was silent but for the tramping of guards on the battlements. A heron perched on a rotting log to watch as they forded the northern meander of the Minfolin. If it found them curious it gave no sign, but flapped heavily as the white spray flew from trotting hooves.

Dissolution Kahn rode in the lead with wry pride, his massive frame clad in mail lacquered cobalt blue. Over the mail he wore a silk surcoat of the same acid yellow as his mare's caparisons. He had relinquished his rustic hat, and his mane of blond hair blew back in the light wind. At his side was a great broadsword with a silver-bound hilt. The roan mare arched her powerful neck, shook her delicate head. Her bridle was of soft red leather, with a subtle leather filigree inlaid.

To tegeus-Cromis, hunched against the morning chill on a somber black gelding, wrapped in his crow-cloak, it seemed that the Kahn and his horse threw back the light like a challenge: for a moment, they were heraldic and invincible, the doom to which they traveled something beautiful and unguessed. But the emotion was brief, and passed.

As he went, his seat insecure on a scruffy packhorse, his only armor a steel-stressed leather cap, Rotgob the dwarf chanted a Rivermouth song of forgotten meaning, "The Dead Freight Dirge:

Burn them up and sow them deep,
Oh, drive them down!
Heavy weather in the Fleet,
Oh, drive them down!
Gather them up and drive them down,
Oh, sow them deep!
Driving wind and plodding feet,
Oh, *drive them down!*

And as the ritualistic syllables rolled, Cromis found himself sinking into a reverie of death and spoliation, haunted by gray, translucent images of the dead merchant in his desecrated chamber, of telescopes and strange astrologies. The face of the woman in the hooded purple cloak hung before him, in the grip of some deep but indefinable sorrow. He was aware of the Marsh somewhere up ahead, embodiment of his peculiar destiny and his unbearable heritage.

He was receding from the world, as if the cocaine fit were on him and all his anchor chains were cut, when Kahn reined in his mare and called them to a halt.

"There's our way. The Beast has left the road here, as you see."

A narrow track ran east from the road. Fifty yards along it, the bracken and gorse of the valley failed and the terrain became brown, faintly iridescent bog, streaked with slicks

of purple and oily yellow. Beyond that rose thickets of
strangely shaped trees. The river meandered through it, slow
and broad, flanked by dense reedbeds of a bright ocher
color. The wind blew from the east, carrying a bitter, metallic smell.

"Some might find it beautiful," said Cromis.

Where the bracken petered out a dike had been sunk to
prevent the herd animals of the Low Leedale from wandering
into the bog. It was deep and steep-sided, full of stagnant
water over which lay a multicolored film of scum. They
crossed by a gated wooden bridge, the hooves of their horses
clattering hollowly.

"I don't," said Rotgob the dwarf. "It stinks."

3

Deep in the Marsh, the path wound tortuously between
umber iron bogs, albescent quicksands of aluminum and
magnesium oxides, and sumps of cuprous blue or perman-
ganate mauve fed by slow gelid streams and fringed by
silver reeds. The trees were smooth-barked, yellow-ocher
and burnt-orange; through their tightly woven foliage filtered a gloomy light. At their roots grew tall black grasses
and great clumps of multifaceted transparent crystals, like
alien fungi.

Charcoal-gray frogs with viridescent eyes croaked as they
floundered between the pools. Beneath the greasy surface
of the water unidentifiable reptiles moved slowly and sin-
uously. Dragonflies whose webby wings spanned a foot or
more hummed and hovered between the sedges: their long
wicked bodies glittered bold green and ultramarine; they
took their prey on the wing, pouncing with an audible snap
of jaws on whining ephemera and fluttering moths of april
blue and chevrolet cerise.

Over everything hung the oppressive stench of rotting metal. After an hour, Cromis's mouth was coated by a bitter deposit, and he tasted acids. He found it difficult to speak. While his horse slithered and stumbled beneath him, he gazed about in wonder, and poetry moved in his skull, swift as the jeweled mosquito-hawks over a dark slow current of ancient decay.

He drove Rotgob and the Kahn hard, sensing the imminence of his meeting with the *baan* now that the blood-trail had vanished and they followed a line of big, shapeless impressions in the mud. But the horses were reluctant, confused by prussian streams and fragile organic-pink sky. At times, they refused to move, bracing their legs and trembling. They turned rolling white eyes on their owners, who cursed and sank to their boot tops in the slime, releasing huge acrid bubbles of gas.

When they emerged from the trees for a short while about noon, Cromis noticed that the true sky was full of racing, wind-torn clouds; and despite its exotic colors, the Marsh was cold.

By the evening of that day, they were still on the hunt, and had reached the shallow waters of Cobaltmere in the northern reaches of the Marsh. They had lost one pack-pony to the shifting sands; the other had died painfully after drinking from a deceptively clear pool, its limbs swelling up and blood pouring from its corroded internal organs. They were tired and filthy, and they had lost the beast's spoor.

They made camp in a fairly dry clearing halfway round the waterlogged ambit of the mere. Far out on the water lay fawn mudbanks streaked with sudden yellow, and floating islands of matted vegetation on which waterbirds cackled, ruffling their electric-blue feathers. As the day decayed, the colors were numbed, but in the funereal light of sunset the water of the Cobaltmere came alive with mile-long stains of cochineal and mazarine.

Cromis was awaked some time before dawn by what he
assumed to be the cold. A dim disturbing phosphorescence
of fluctuating color hung over the mere and its environs;
caused by some odd quality of the water there, it gave an
even but wan light. There were no shadows. Trees loomed
vague and damp at the periphery of the clearing.

When he found it impossible to sleep again, he moved
nearer to the dead embers of the fire. He lay there uneasily,
wrapped in blanket and cloak, his fingers laced beneath his
head, staring up at the Name Stars and the enigmatic Group.

Beside him humped the Kahn, snoring. The horses shifted
drowsily. A nocturnal mosquito-hawk with huge obsidian
globes for eyes hunted over the shallows, humming and
snapping. He watched it for a moment, fascinated, the sound
of water draining through the reedbeds. Rotgob was on
watch: he moved slowly round the clearing and out of
Cromis's field of vision, blowing warmth into his cupped
hands, cursing as his feet sank with soft noises into the
earth.

Cromis closed his eyes, depressed, insomniac. He wondered if the Sixth Beast had reserved its role. Incidents of
such a reversal filtered up to him from the dim, haunted
library stacks of his youth, where his doomed father had
taught him harsh lore: black-lettered spines and a pale woman
he had always wanted to know.

He thought of the woman in the hooded purple cloak as
he had first seen her.

He heard a faint sigh behind him: not close, and too low-
pitched to wake a sleeping man, but of peculiar strength
and urgency.

Fear gnawed him, and he could not suppress sudden
images of his father's corpse and its return to the libraries.

He felt for the hilt of the nameless sword. Finding it, he
rolled cautiously onto his stomach, making as little unnec-

essary movement as possible and breathing through his open mouth. This maneuver brought into view the segment of the clearing previously invisible to him. He studied the point from which the sound had come.

The glade was quiet and ghastly. A dark wound marked its entrance. The horses issued breath or ectoplasm. One of them had cocked its ears forward alertly.

He could neither hear nor see the dwarf.

Carefully, he freed himself from his blanket, eased his sword a few inches from its scabbard. Reflex impelled him to crouch low as he ran across the clearing. When he encountered the corpse of the dwarf, he recognized a little of the horror that had lived with him under the guise of ennui since the death of his father.

Small and huddled, Rotgob had already sunk slightly into the wet ground. There was no blood apparent, and his limbs were uncut. He had not drawn his long stiletto.

Clasping the cold, stubbled jaw, his skin crawled with revulsion. The dwarf snarled—unlike the merchant, unembarrassed in the presence of death. His fingers, though, were all in a knot. Cromis moved the head, and the neck was unbroken, hard to flex. The skull, then. He probed reluctantly, withdrew his fingers, clasped his head in his hands, and, recovering, wiped his face with the edge of his cloak.

On his feet, swallowing bile, he shivered. The night was silent but for the far-off sleepless hum of a dragonfly. The earth around the corpse was poached and churned. Big, shapeless impressions led out of the glade to the south. He followed them, swaying, without waking the Kahn.

It was a personal thing with him.

Away from the Cobaltmere, the phosphorescence faded. He followed the tracks swiftly. They left the path at a place where the trees were underlit by clumps of pale blue crystal. Bathed in an unsteady glow, he stopped to strain his ears.

Nothing but the sound of water. It occurred to him that he was alone. The earth sucked his feet. The trees were weird, their boughs a frozen writhe.

To the left, a branch snapping.

He whirled, threw himself into the undergrowth, hacking out with the nameless sword. At each step he sank into the muck; small animals scuttled away from him; foliage clutched his limbs.

He stood breathing heavily in a tiny clearing with a dangerous pool. After a minute, he could hear nothing; after two, nothing more.

"If I'd come alone the first encounter would have been the last. Go home, Kahn, please. Or to Duirinish, and wait for me."

They buried the dwarf before dawn, working in the odd light of Cobaltmere. Dissolution Kahn wrapped his dead friend's fingers round the thing that was neither a short sword nor a long stiletto. "You never know where you might find a dark alley." He seemed to bear Cromis no grudge for the death, but dug silently, putting in more effort than the earth warranted.

"The dwarf was a good fighter. He killed four Princes"—this, he repeated absently, twice—"I'll stay with it until we've finished the job."

The temperature had been dropping steadily for hours. A few brittle flakes of snow filtered through the colorful foliage, out of context. Lord tegeus-Cromis huddled into his cloak, touched the turned earth with his foot.

He thought of the high passes of Monar, suffocating in snow.

"Kahn, you don't understand. History is against you. The Sixth House . . . The responsibility is mine. By sharing it, I've killed three people instead of one. . . ."

The Kahn spat.

"I'll stay with it."

Later, sucking bits of food from his mustache, he said: "You take a single setback too hard. Have some cooked pig? There are still two of us."

From the eyots and reedbeds, fowl cackled: sensing a change, they were gathering in great multicolored drifts on the surface of the lake, slow migratory urges climaxing in ten thousand small, dreary skulls.

Cromis laughed dully.

He took out his pewter snuffbox and stared at it. "Snow, Kahn," he murmured. "A grain of snow." He shrugged. "Or two." He undid the box.

The Kahn reached out and knocked it from his hand.

"That won't help," he said pleasantly.

Only half was spilt, and perhaps half of that spoiled. Cromis scooped the rest up, closed the box carefully. Then he stood and brushed the filth from his knees.

"Your mother," he said, "was a sow." He let the Kahn see a few inches of the nameless sword. "She gave men diseases."

"How you found out is a mystery to me. Come on, Lord Cromis, it's dawn."

The snow held off for a while.

4

"Nobody has been here for a hundred years."

At the extreme northwestern edge of the Marsh, where the concentration of metal salts washed off the Rust Desert, low, saner vegetation had taken hold: willow drooped over the watercourses, the reedbeds were cream and brown, creaking in the cold wind. But the malformations were of a subtler and more disturbing kind—something in the stance of the trees, the proportion of the interface insects—and there was no great lessening of the gloom.

"A pity. Had the place been charted, we might have come to it directly and saved—"

"—A life?"

"Some trouble."

An ancient roundtower reared above the trees. Built of fawn stone at some time when the earth was firmer, it stood crookedly, weathered like an old bone. Filaments of dead ivy crawled over it; blackthorn and alder hid its base; a withered bullace grew from an upper window, its rattling branches inhabited by small, stealthy birds.

Closing on it, they found that its lower stories were embedded in the earth: the low, rectangular openings spaced evenly around its damp walls were foundered windows. Three or four feet above the muck it was girdled by a broad band of fungus, like ringworm on the limb of an unhealthy man.

"My father's books hinted at the existence of a sinking tower, but placed it in the east."

"You could live to correct them."

"Perhaps." Cromis urged his horse forward, drew his sword. Birds fled the blackthorn. Snow had begun to fall again, the flakes softer this time, and larger. "Are we fool-hardy to approach so openly?"

The Kahn got off his long roan mare and studied the deep, clumsy spoor of the *baan*. An avenue of broken branches and crushed sedge ended in a patch of trampled ground before one of the sunken windows, as if the thing grew careless in the security of its lair. He scratched his head.

"Yes."

He gazed at the tower and said nothing for some minutes. Gray snow eddied about his motionless figure, settled briefly in his beard. His cloak flapped and cracked in the wind, and he fingered the hilt of his broadsword uneasily. He went a little nearer the dark opening. He paced backward from it. Finally, he said:

"I'm afraid I can't get in there; it's too small."

Cromis nodded.

"You'll keep watch."

"I would come if I could. You are mad if you do it alone."

Cromis took off his cloak.

"There is already a thing between us unsettled. Don't add another one. There is no onus on you. Watch my back."

Visibility had dropped to ten paces. Glimpsed through a shifting white curtain, the Kahn's face was expressionless; but his eyes were bemused and hurt. Cromis threw his cloak over the hindquarters of his shivering horse, then turned and walked quickly to the sunken window. Snow was already gathering on its lintel. He felt the Kahn's eyes on him.

"Leave now!" he shouted into the wind. "It doesn't want you!"

He got down on his hands and knees, trying to keep the nameless sword pointed ahead of him. A queer mixture of smells bellied out of the slot into his face: the stink of rotting dung, overlayed by a strong, pleasant musk.

He coughed. Against his will, he hung back. He heard the Kahn call out from a long way off. Ashamed, he thrust his head into the hole, wriggled frantically through.

It was dark, and nothing met him.

He tried to stand; halfway upright, he hit his head on the damp ceiling. Doors for dwarfs, he thought, doors for dwarfs. Cold, foul liquid dripped into his hair and down his cheek. He crouched, began to stumble about, thrusting with his sword and sobbing unpleasant challenges. His feet slid on a soft and rotten surface; he fell. The sword struck orange sparks from a wall.

He conceived a terrible fear of something behind him.

He danced, made a bitter stroke.

The lair was empty.

He dropped his sword and wept.

"I didn't ask for this!" he told his childhood, but it was lost among the library stacks, learning ways to kill the Beast. "I didn't *ask* to come here!"

He lay in the dung, groping about; he clasped the blade of the sword and lacerated the palm of his hand. He squirmed through the window, out into the blind snow.

"Kahn!" he shouted. "Kahn!"

He stood up, using the sword as a crutch. Blood ran down it. He took a few uncertain steps, looking for the horses. They were gone.

He ran three times round the base of the building, crying out. Confused by the snow—settling on the trees, it produced harsh contrasts, further distorting the landscape—he had difficulty locating his starting point. The accident with the sword had left three of his fingers useless; the tendons were cut. After he had rubbed some cocaine into the wound and bound it up, he went to look for the Kahn.

A layer of gray, greasy slush had formed on the ground. Bent forward against the weather, he picked up two sets of hoofprints leading back toward the Cobaltmere.

He looked back once at the sinking tower. High up on its southern face a group of windows were eroded, indistinct edges regarded him sympathetically. Snow gathered on his shoulders; he blundered into sumps and streams; he lost the trail and found it again. The pain in his hand receded to a great distance. He began to snicker gently at his experiences in the lair of the Beast.

The wildfowl were gone from Cobaltmere. He stood by a fast purple watercourse and caught glimpses through the snow of long vacant sandbanks and reefs. He went down to the water. His horse was lying there, its head in the mere,

its body swollen, his cloak still wrapped and tangled round
its hindquarters. Blood oozed from its mouth and anus. The
veins in its eyes were yellow.

He heard a faint, fading cry above the sound of the wind.

5

Dissolution Kahn sat on his pink roan mare in a somber
clearing by the water.

Melting snow had washed his splendid mail of the filth
of the Marsh, and he held his sword high above his head.
The mare's silk caparisons gleamed against a claustrophobic
backdrop. She arched her neck, shook her delicate head,
and her breath steamed. The Kahn's hair blew back like a
pennant, and he was laughing.

To tegeus-Cromis, forcing his way through a stand of
mutated willows that clutched desperately at his clothes, it
seemed that the glade could not contain them: they had
passed beyond it into heraldry, and were invincible.

And although the Sixth Beast was intimately his, he
gained no clear image of it as it loomed above man and
horse.

Shaking its plumage irritably, it broke wind and lifted a
clawed paw to scratch a suppurating place on its pachy-
dermal hide. Chitinous scales rattled like dead reeds. It
roared and whistled sardonically, winked a heavy lid over
one insectile eye, did a clumsy dance of sexual lust on its
hind hooves, writhed its coils in stupid menace.

It tried to form words.

It laughed delightedly, lifted a wing, and preened. A
pleasant musk filled the glade. It reached for the doomed
man on his beautiful horse with long brittle fingers.

It said distinctly:

"I am a liar as well as a dwarf."

It sent a hot stream of urine into the sodden earth.

It increased it size by a factor or two, staggered, giggled, regained its balance, and fell at the Kahn.

Cromis dragged himself free of the willows and ran into the glade, yelling, "Run, Kahn, run!"

Blood spattered the roan mare's caparisons.

Dissolution Kahn vomited suddenly, clinging to his saddle as the horse reared. He recovered, swung his weapon in a wide arc. He grunted, swayed. The Beast overshadowed him. He stabbed it.

It howled.

"NO!" pleaded Cromis.

"No!" moaned the Beast.

It began to diminish.

Kahn sat the mare with his head bowed. He dropped his sword. His mail was in shreds; here and there, strips of it were embedded in his flesh.

Before him the Sixth Beast of Viriconium, the mutable Lamia, shriveled, shedding wings and scales. Every facet of its eyes went dull. "Please," it said. A disgusting stink blew away on the wind. Certain of its limbs had withered away, leaving warty stumps. Iridescent fluids mixed with the water of the Marsh. Its mouths clicked feebly.

A little later, when the corpse of the Beast, having repeated all its incarnations, had attained its final shrunken form, the Kahn looked up. His face was pouchy and lined. He slid out of the saddle, wearily slapped the mare's neck. The snow eased off, stopped.

He looked at Cromis. He might never have seen him before. He jerked his thumb at the corpse.

"You should have killed her at the inn," he said.

He stumbled backward. His mouth fell open. When he

looked down and saw the nameless sword protruding from
his lower belly, he whimpered. A quick, violent shudder
went through him. Blood dribbled down his thighs. He
reached down slowly and put his hands on the sword.

"Why?"

"It was mine, Kahn. The Beast was mine to kill. It's
dead, but I'm still alive. I never expected this. What can I
do now?"

Dissolution Kahn sat down carefully, still holding the
sword. He coughed and wiped his mouth.

"Give me some of that cocaine. I could still make it out
of here."

Abruptly, he laughed.

"You were gulled," he said bitterly, "every one of you.
Your ancestors were all gulled.

"It was easy to kill. You spent your lives in misery, but
it was *easy*. How do you feel about that? Please give me
some of that stuff."

"What will I do?" whispered Cromis.

Dissolution Kahn twisted round until he faced the corpse
of the woman in the hooded purple cloak. He leant forward,
steadied the pommel of the nameless sword against her ribs,
and pushed himself onto it. He groaned.

Lord tegeus-Cromis sat in the glade until evening, the
little pewter snuffbox on his knees. He saw nothing. Eventually he pulled the nameless sword from the Kahn's belly
and threw it into the mere.

He swung himself onto the long roan mare, wrapped the
dead man's cloak around him.

On his way out of the clearing he contemplated the final
avatar of Lamia the Beast.

"You should have killed me that first night at the inn,"
he said. On an impulse he dismounted, took the clasp of

her cloak. "Lady, you should have done it."

He rode north all night, and when he came from under the trees of the Marsh he avoided looking up, in case the Name Stars should reflect some immense and unnatural change below.

Lamia Mutable

Track One: At the Bistro Californium.

THE BURNING TAKES place next day, on an amethyst and emerald lifting-platform, high up in gray turbulent air, drifting. The gathered crowd—in Happy-Day motley: yellow pantaloons, jewels, flame-red saris—roars and whispers, an inland sea of laughter, as oily smoke begins to rise from the gaudy pyre. Birkin Grif and Lamia, the woman without skin, are amused but unimpressed.

"I was burned at Pompeii in such a jeweled gown. Man, these plebs have missed much, having been lost all these puritan centuries." Her dentures twinkle, her beautiful arteries pulse. Birkin Grif eyes her patronizingly: skinless, she is not nude but naked, more naked ever than a woman can be when merely divested of clothes. He possesses her every function with his single eye, piratical.

"True," says he. "But Gomorrah was best; there was a good burning there." She laughs, and her laugh is naked too. Sparks issue from the gemmed platform to an appreciative roar from the crowd. Birkin Grif slaps his titanium thigh in huge enjoyment.

"Jeanne d'Arc," says the skinless woman.

"Hiroshima," he counters.

"Virgil Grissom," she laughs.

"Buchenwald," murmurs Birkin Grif.

Lost in delightful reminiscence, they watch the platform with its cargo of burning emperor, two ancient lovers in a crowd, he old with debauchery, she young with it. A drunken woman, her head bejeweled from crown to forehead, staggers from the press.

"Whoop!"

"Indeed, madam," says Birkin Grif, always the wag. "Were you not at Nagasaki in the spring? Did I not see you there?" The drunken woman narrows her eyes.

"How d'you spell it, baby?"

Birkin Grif ogles her with his good eye.

"G-U-I-L-T," he intimates.

Skinless Lamia sniffs petulantly and nudges him in the ribs.

"Why are we here? Why are we here at all? This is not where it's at. We have a date in Californium."

They leave the crowd to heave and sweat. The platform is being lowered so that the burning emperor's retinue of harlots can be put aboard. Birkin Grif limps plausibly; his skinless sweetheart is a distillate of timeworn nakedness: false teeth and bijou eyebrows her slight concessions to fashion.

Pause the First.

Welcome to the chrome-plastic uterus of the Bistro Californium, haunt well-beloved and dear watering place of all the intellectual parodies and artistic mock-ups of the splendid city.

See: here is Kristodulos, the blind painter; a brush dipped in cochineal is placed behind his ear. He is listening to the color of his Negress, Charmian, with the scarred ritual breasts. Here too is Adolf Ableson (Junior), the spastic poet of Viriconium. See how his chromium hand grips the pencil with metallic fervor, how his head nods, driven by some bent escapement in his neck. And here, here at *this* table, thirsting after the hungry snows, here is Jiro-San, the hermaphrodite lute-player—shut up in a tower of loneliness, separated by the accusation of mutability from Mistress Seng, she of the lapis-lazuli eyes—carven, nay (no no no) graven, from a bronze sunburn.

O you pedestrian seekers-after-color: come, gaze. . . .

Enter Birkin Grif and Lamia, his skinless lover. They sit at a table of translucent rose glass, wink and nod knowingly at companions-in-knowingness. Faintly, the whisper of the crowd at the Incineration sifts into the Bistro Californium, soft little flakes of sound. Kristodulos colors it black, makes a mental note. The chromium poet scribbles *and having writ, moves on*. Only our lute-player is deaf, because— suntanned—he is occupied with his head full of snow.

"Shall we take tea?"

Smiling, they take tea out of gold-leaved porcelain.

TRACK TWO: WHO IS DR. GRISHKIN?

"It is I will conduct you."

Birkin Grif looks up. This voice owns a fat and oily face, faintly gray. In the face is placed with artistic but ungeometrical accuracy, a small rosebud mouth, attempting to beam. One understands immediately that the mouth is indigenous to this kind of face, but that the smile is not. There are violet oblique eyes; no eyebrows or hair. The voice has a body too: pear-shaped, draped in plum-colored suiting, and very plump. The plum-colored suit is slit to reveal a surgical window set into its owner's stomach. Behind the window, interesting things are happening.

This voice—along with its corpus—is the essence of every brothel and fornication of the universe: the voice of a glorious, immortal, and galactic pimp; the ultimate in carnal, carnival, and carnivorous invitations.

"My friend," says Birkin Grif. "Mon ami: have I not seen you before? A whorehouse in Alexandria? Istanbul? Birmingham? No?" The newcomer smiles with a sort of lecherous modesty.

"Perhaps . . . ah, but that was a millennium hence. We have progressed since then. We have become . . . civilized." He shrugs.

"Does it matter?" asks Birkin Grif.

"Nothing matters, my piratical friend. But that is not the point: I am Dr. Grishkin."

"Is *that* the point?"

"No, that is something altogether different. May I join you?"

And he sits down, leering at the woman without skin. This is a leer that makes her *feel* naked. There is a hiatus. He pours himself tea. He has a strong sense of drama, this Dr. Grishkin: he is well-versed in the technique of the dramatic pause. Birkin Grif becomes impatient.

"Dr. Grishkin, we . . ."

Grishkin raises an admonitory finger. He sips tea. He points to his surgical window. Birkin Grif watches it, fascinated.

"The ash-flats," intones Dr. Grishkin and, having dropped his conversational bomb, sits back to watch its effect.

Horror. Silence. Tension drips viscous from the Californium ceiling. Far off, the crowd whispers. Nothing so dramatic has happened in Californium for a decade.

"I am to take you to the ash-flats of Wisdom."

Skinless Lamia shudders ever so slightly. Into the silence

fall three perfect silver notes. Jiro-San has taken up his lute.

"I think I have changed my mind," she whispers.

"It is too late; all is arranged," says Dr. Grishkin. "You must come now: it is inevitable that you come." There is the slightest edge of annoyance to his voice. This annoyance is persuasive. One feels that Dr. Grishkin has gone to much trouble to... bring things about. He does not wish to be disappointed.

"But will He be there?" asks Birkin Grif anxiously. "There is little sense in risking so much if He is not there."

Comes the answer: "There is little sense in anything, Mr. Grif. But He will be there. He has sent me." He sips tea. It is so simple, the way he puts it, it seems already an accomplished fact; but then, his oily job is to simplify, to smooth the way. Lamia leans forward, speaks from the corner of her mouth, the perfect conspirator. Dr. Grishkin finds her skinned proximity delightfully disturbing, her aorta distinctly beautiful.

"The Image-Police, Dr. Grishkin: what of them?"

"Pure paranoia, dear lady. There is nothing *very* illegal about a little trip to the edge of Wisdom. Just to the *edge*, you understand, merely a sight-seeing trip: a little pleasant tourism...." He leers. "Shall we go?"

They leave. The fat man waddles. Birkin limps. The skinless lady is sinuous. As they pass Jiro-San's table, he gazes wistfully. He finds Birkin very handsome.

Track Three: The Ash-Flats of Wisdom.

Wisdom is a wilderness. Long ago, there was a war here; or perhaps it was a peace. Most of the time there is but small difference between the two; love and hate lean so heavily upon one another, and both are possessed of a monstrous ennui. Certainly, something destroyed whatever Wisdom was: so well that no one has known its former nature for two centuries. From its border one can see little, but sense much.

Birkin Grif and the skinless woman stand shivering there in a cold wind, peering through the mesh fence that separates city-ground and forbidden ash. Their cloaks—black for him, gray for her—flutter nervously. Soft flakes of ash fill the air about them with dark snow. Grishkin is huge in voluminous purple, talking animatedly to a gray-faced guard outside his olive-drab sentry box. Meanwhile, the desolation seems to whisper, *You have no business here; everything here is dead.*

There is a bleak sadness to this waste, a bereavement: it mourns. Eidetic images of ghosts flit on this wind: women weeping weave shrouds at ebb tide; famine-children wail to old men at twilight. Here there are two kinds of chill, and cloaks will not keep out both.

Abruptly, Grishkin takes out a small silver mechanism and points it at the guard. There is an incredible blue flash. The body of the guard drops, improbably headless, jetting dark blood from the venturi of its neck. Dr. Grishkin vomits apologetically: a sick valediction. He returns, wiping his mouth on a canary-yellow handkerchief.

"You see? There is no problem, as I have said." He retches, his fat face white. "Oh dear. Excuse me, do excuse me. *I grow old, I grow old,* you know. Poor boy. He has a mother in Australia. He was exported."

"How sad," says Lamia. She is gazing at Dr. Grishkin's heaving stomach through the surgical window. She feels quite sympathetic. "Sympathy is so quaint," she tinkles. "Poor Dr. Grishkin."

Poor Dr. Grishkin, his spasm over, takes out his little glittering mechanism again, and aims it at the fence round Wisdom. The incredible-blue-flash performance is repeated, whereupon the mesh curls and congeals like burning hair.

"Pretty," observes the skinless woman.

"Impressive," admits Birkin Grif. In the charred sentry box bells begin to ring.

"Now we must hurry," intimates Dr. Grishkin, and his voice is more than faintly urgent. "Leg it!" He begins to waddle hurriedly toward a charcoal dune. They follow him through the broken mesh. The wind rises, whipping up small, stinging cinders. Cloaks fluttering, they top the rise and drop flat, facing the way they have come. A great turmoil of ash-flakes hides the sentry box.

"The wind will have erased our tracks," says Birkin Grif.

"Correct as ever, *mon frère,*" returns fat Dr. Grishkin. "Officially, we have just died; nobody will bother us now." He leers. "I have been dead these ten years." He laughs mordantly. His stomach trembles behind its window. Birkin Grif and his skinless mistress are unamused.

"Why does the ash never blow into the city?" asks Lamia.

"Come," orders Grishkin, eyeing the weather with distaste.

PAUSE THE SECOND.
FOR NARRATIVE PURPOSES THE ASH STORM ABATES.

Led by the seraphic murderer Grishkin, they flit like majestic moths—purple, gray, black—over the long low swells of ash.

This land is empty, composed visually of utterly balanced sweeps of gray, shading from the dead cream to the mystic charcoal. Slow watercourses cut the ubiquitous ash, silting swiftly, meandering, beds infinitely variable. Wind and water make Wisdom unchartable: age and the wind make it cripplingly lonely. Time is overthrown in Wisdom: its very mutability is immutable.

Thinks Birkin Grif: *This land is the ultimate vision of*

the Ab-real Eternity. Across it we scuttle like three symbolic beetles without legs.

TRACK FOUR: I REMEMBER CORINTH.

Flitting minutiae on the broad back of the waste, they finally achieve their heroic goal.

Dr. Grishkin stops.

He and Birkin Grif and the skinless woman stand—at the end of the erratic line of footprints—at the apparent center of an immense, featureless plain: the hub of a massive stasis, a vast silence. The horizon has vanished; there is no obvious convergence of ash and sky: both are flat monochrome gray. Because of this, environment is shapeless; dimensions are unclear; the three suddenly exist without proper frame of reference, with the sole and inadequate orientation of their own bodies. The effect confuses; they become dream figures on a back-cloth of ab-space: unattached, divested of every vestige of their accepted and appropriate reality.

"It is here we must wait," says Dr. Grishkin, his fat voice devoid of expression, drained of expression by the single-tone emptiness.

"But He is not here. . . ." begins Birkin Grif, fighting to prevent the visual null from sucking up his very thoughts, speaking precisely only through mammoth effort.

"We must wait," repeats Grishkin.

"Will He come, though?" demands Grif thickly, struggling with the silence. "If this is a fool's errand . . ." His implied threat falls flat, negated by the vacuum.

"You have lived a fool's errand for a millennium: why quibble now? Here we wait." Slow steel in Grishkin's voice; again he will not be denied. They wait. At this point of minimal orientation, without movement or sound, it seems that eons pass. They wait. Nothing happens for a million years. Finally, Grif speaks, his words harsh and congested with a sudden aged, neurotic ferocity. "I think I may kill you, Dr. Grishkin. He is not coming. All the way to nowhere, and He is not coming. I think I will kill you...." His face is distorted; his good eye winks, manic; this is a senile fury.

"Shut up." Grishkin is smiling his rosebud parody. "Shut up and look!"

"...I think I will *kill* you...." hisses Grif, like a machine running down fixedly through a series of programmed spasms. But he looks.

Skinless Lamia is dancing on the ash, magnificently naked once more. Her feet make no sound. She moves to a muted hum of her own making; an insistent, droning raga. She dances possessed, smiling in introspective wonder at her own movement, antithesis of the greater stillness. Her dance is a final destruction of orientation: almost, she floats.

And she is *changing*.

"Is this not the ultimate in body-schema illusions?" breathes Grishkin. "See: she is *living* her hallucination!" He is quite overtly touched by the poetry of it all.

Her body elongates...contracts...flows...diminishes. A tail appears, flips archly, disappears. A jeweled dolphin exists whole for an instant, dissolves. The modal hum rises and falls. A golden salamander weaves, sloughs off its skin...becomes a bright proud bird, falters, shimmering at its edges...disembodies reluctantly....

By turns the plastic Lamia is fish, fowl, and beast, myth and dream. Then one shape steadies—

And Lamia is no more.

Dr. Grishkin releases his breath in one long sigh of artistic pleasure. Birkin Grif screams.

For, on the ash—cinders and dust adhering to its wet membrane—there lies a live human fetus.

It kicks a little, stretching the membrane. . . .

Birkin Grif retches and moans: "Oh, my God . . . what . . . ?"

Dr. Grishkin is apologetic but unhelpful. "Don't ask me, Grif, *mon vieux*. I expected a snake. But, oh, what poetry; such a metamorphosis!" The fetus jerks. Grif whirls on Dr. Grishkin, hysterical, whining like a child.

"Cheat! Liar! This is not what we came here for. This is not it at all. You have cheated . . . it isn't fair!"

Coldly, Grishkin, galactic pimp extraordinary, appraises him. His pleasure is quite gone away. His eyes impale the blubbering Grif.

"Fair? *You* have yet to learn the rules of the game! Fair?" Grif is pinned to the inert landscape by those bleak, oblique eyes. "There is no fairness to inevitability. This was inevitable, Mr. Birkin Grif—inevitable because it has happened. Accept it because of that. Do not look to me for *fairness*." He finds the word distasteful. He pauses to gaze speculatively at the drying fetus.

Then: "You expect too much, ˙my friend. You desire, and expect the universe to provide. But that is not the way of things. No indeed." He appears pleased with this summary. Then he frowns suddenly, as if rediscovering an unpleasant reality. "It is a pity you have learned so late. *Too* late, in point of fact."

And his glittering, malevolent little device is out in a microsecond, as Birkin Grif throws himself frantically forward, horrid realization contorting his features. Thus dies Grif, last of the archetypal sybarites, while the fetus of his skinless lover lies twitching on the ground. He scarcely has time for a second scream.

His enigmatic slayer shrugs and turns to the feebly struggling fetus. Gazing, he shakes his hairless head. Such poetry. Reluctantly, he steps on it. For all his sensibility, he has a tidy mind. Casting a last glance at the smoking Birkin Grif—titanium thigh his sole remnant of personality—Dr.

Grishkin, the Bringer with the Window, pulls his purple cloak around him and waddles off.

Soon, only his footprints are left on the ash-flats of Wisdom.

Viriconium Knights

THE BRAVOS OF THE High City whistle to one another all night as they go about their grim factional games among the derelict observatories and abandoned fortifications at Lowth. Sometimes desultory and distant, sometimes shockingly close at hand, these shrill exchanges—short, peremptory blasts interspersed with the protracted, wailing responses which always seem to end on an interrogative note—form the basis of a complicated language. You wake suddenly to their echo in the leaden hours before dawn. When you go to the window the street below is empty. You may hear running footsteps, or an urgent sigh. After a minute or two the whistles move away in the direction of the Tinmarket or the Margarethestrasse. Next morning some minor lordling is discovered in the gutter with his throat cut, and all you are left with is the impression of a secret war, a lethal patience, a quiet maneuvering in the dark.

The children of the Quarter pretend to understand these signals. They know the names of all the most desperate men in the city. In the mornings on their way to the Lycee on Simeonstrasse they scrutinize every lined, exhausted face, every meal-colored cloak, every man with a sword and soft shoes who swaggers past on the Boulevard Aussman.

"There goes Antic Horn," they whisper, "master of the Blue Anemone Philosophical Association." And: "Last night Osgerby Practal killed two of the Queen's men right underneath my window. He did it with his knife—like this!— and then whistled the 'found and killed' of the Locust Clan. . . ."

If you had followed the whistles one raw evening in December some years after the War of the Two Queens, they would have led you to an infamous cobbled yard behind the inn called The Dryad's Saddle at the junction of Rue Miromesnil and Salt Pie Lane. The sun had gone down an hour before, under three bars of ragged orange cloud. Wet snow had been falling since. Smoke and steam drifted from the inn in the light of a half-open door; there was a sharp smell in the air, compounded of embrocation, saveloys, and burning coal. The yard was crowded on three sides with men whose woolen cloaks were dyed at the hem the color of dried blood, men who stood with the braced instep affected only by swordsmen and dancers. They were quiet and intent, and for the most part ignored the laughter that came from the inn.

Long ago someone had set four wooden posts into the yard. Blackened and still, capped with snow, they formed a square fifteen or twenty feet on a side. Half a dozen apprentices were at work to clear the square, using long-handled brooms to sweep away the slush and blunted trowels to chip at the hardened ridges of ice left by the previous day's encounters.

(By day these lads sell sugared anemones in the Rivelin Market. They run errands for the card sharps. But in the afternoon their eyes become distant, thoughtful, excited; and at night they put on their loose, girlish woolen jackets and tight leather breeches to become the handlers and nurses of the men who wear the meal-colored cloaks. What are we to make of them? They are thin and ill-fed, but so devout.

They walk with a light tread. Even their masters do not understand them.)

A gray-haired man sat on a stool among the members of his faction while two apprentices prepared him. They had taken off his cloak and his mail shirt, and strapped up his right wrist with a wide leather thong. They had pulled back the hair from his heavy face and fastened it with an ornamental steel clasp. Now they were rubbing embrocation into his stiff shoulder muscles. He ignored them, staring emptily at the combat square where the blackened posts waited for him like corpses pulled out of a bog. He showed no sign that he felt the cold, though his bare arms, covered in thick old scars, were purple with it. Once he inserted two fingers beneath the strapping on his wrist to make sure it was tight enough. His sword was propped up against his knees. Idly he pushed the point of it down between two cobblestones and began to lever them apart.

One of the apprentices leaned forward and whispered something in his ear. For a moment it appeared he wouldn't answer. Then he cleared his throat as if he had not spoken to anybody for a long time.

"I've never heard of him," he said. "And anyway, why should I be frightened of some stripling from Mynned?"

The boy smiled calmly down at him.

"I will always follow you, Practal. Even if he cuts your legs off."

Suddenly, without turning round or even moving his head, Practal reached up and grabbed the boy's thin forearm.

"If he kills me you'll run off with the first poseur who comes in here wearing soft shoes and a cloak of the right color!"

"No," said the boy.

Practal held his arm a moment longer, then gave a short laugh. "More fool you," he said, but he seemed to be satisfied. He went back to prizing at the loose cobblestones.

A few minutes later the Queen's man came into the yard from the inn, surrounded by the courtiers in yellow velvet cloaks who had escorted him down from Mynned. Practal studied them briefly and spat on the cobbles. The inn was quiet now. From its half-open door a few latecomers watched, placing bets in low voices while smoke moved slowly in the light and warmth behind them.

The Queen's man ignored Practal. He walked round the combat square, kicking vaguely at each wooden post as he came to it and staring about as if he had forgotten something. He was a tall youth with big, mad-looking eyes and hair which had been cut and dyed so that it stuck up from his head like a crest of scarlet spines. He had on a pale green cloak with an orange lightning flash embroidered on the back; when he took it off the crowd could see that instead of a mail shirt he was wearing a chenille blouse. Practal's faction laughed and pointed. He gazed blankly at them, then with an awkward motion pulled the blouse off and tore it in half. This seemed to annoy the courtiers, who moved away from him and stood in a line along the fourth side of the yard. His chest was thin and white, his back long and hollow. A greenish handkerchief was knotted round his throat. He had as many scars as Practal.

Practal said loudly, "He's a weak-looking thing, then. I wonder why he bothered to come here!"

The Queen's man must have heard this, but he went on lurching randomly about, chewing on something he had in his mouth. Then he scratched his queer coxcomb violently, knelt down, and rummaged through his discarded garments until he came up with a ceramic sheath about a foot long. When the crowd saw this there was some excited betting, most of it against Practal; Practal's faction looked uneasy. Hissing through his teeth as if he were soothing a horse, the Queen's man jerked the power-knife out of its sheath and made a few clumsy passes with it. It gave off a dreary,

lethal buzzing noise and a cloud of pale motes which wobbled away into the wet air like drugged moths; and as it
went it left a sharp line of light behind it in the gloom.

Osgerby Practal shrugged.

"He will need long arms to use that thing," he said.

Someone called out the rules of the fight. As soon as
one of the combatants was cut, he lost. If either of them
stepped outside the square, he would be judged as having
given in. Practal paid no attention. The Queen's man nodded
interestedly as each point was made, then walked off smiling
and whistling.

Practal, who had some experience of mixed fights, kept
his sword back out of the way of the power-knife, partly
to reduce the risk of having it chopped in half, partly so
that his opponent would be encouraged to come to him. The
boy adopted an odd, flat-footed stance, and after a few
seconds of wary circling began to breathe heavily through
his open mouth. Suddenly the power-knife streaked out
between them, fizzing and spitting like a firework. Practal
stepped sideways and let it pass. Before the boy could regain
his balance, Practal had hit him on the top of the head with
the flat of his sword. The boy reeled back with a grunt and
fell against one of the corner posts, biting his underlip and
blinking.

The courtiers clicked their tongues impatiently.

"Come out of that corner and show us a fight!" suggested
someone from Practal's faction. There was laughter.

The boy spoke for the first time. "Go home and look
between your wife's legs, comrade," he said. "I think I left
something there last night."

This answer amused the crowd further. He grinned round
at them. Practal moved in very quickly and hit him very
hard at the angle between his shoulder and neck, again with
the flat of the blade. The power-knife fell out of his numbed
hand and started to eat its way into the cobbles an inch from

his foot, making a dull droning noise. He stood there looking down at it and rubbing his neck.

Practal rested the point of his sword against the boy's diaphragm. But the boy refused to look at him; instead, he went on massaging his neck and staring over the heads of the crowd at the door of The Dryad's Saddle, as if he had the idea of going in there for a drink.

Practal lowered the sword and said to the crowd, "If I kill him too quickly you will give me a reputation for murdering children. We will have a rest."

He returned to his stool and sat down with his back to his opponent. His apprentices wiped his face with a towel, murmuring in low voices, and gave him a dented flask from which to wet his mouth. He held it up. "Do you want to share this?" he called over his shoulder.

"No, thanks," said the boy. "Afterward I can drink it all."

There was more laughter. Practal jumped to his feet, knocking over the stool and spilling the wine. "Fair enough, then!" he shouted, his face red. "Come on!" But for a moment nothing happened. The boy had begun to hack with his heel at a ridge of hard old ice the apprentices had left sticking to the cobbles in the center of the square. The power-knife, held negligently close to his right leg, flickered and sent up whitish motes which floated above the crowd giving off a sickly smell. The boy seemed worried. He kicked repeatedly at the ice, and when he couldn't get it to shift, took an uncertain pace or two forward.

"This square has been badly prepared," he said.

The courtiers shifted irritably. The crowd jeered.

"I don't care about that," said Practal and threw himself at the boy, driving him back with a sustained and very positive attack, whirling the sword in an impressive figure of eight so that it flashed and shone in the light from the inn door. Practal's faction cheered and waved their arms.

The boy retreated unsteadily, and when his foot caught the ridge of ice in the center of the square, he fell over with a cry. Practal raised the sword and brought it down hard. The boy smiled. He moved his head quickly out of the way, and with a clang the blade buried itself between two cobblestones. Even as Practal tried to lever it clear the boy reached round behind his legs and cut the tendons at the back of his knee.

Practal let go of the sword and staggered about the square with his mouth open, holding the backs of his legs. The boy got up and followed him about until he collapsed, then knelt down and put his face close to Practal's to make sure he was listening. "My name is Ignace Retz," he said quietly. Practal bit the cobbles. The boy raised his voice so that the crowd could hear. "My name is Ignace Retz, and I daresay you will remember it."

"Kill me," said Practal.

Ignace Retz shook his head. A groan went through the crowd. Retz walked over to the apprentice who was holding Practal's mail shirt and meal-colored cloak. "I will need a new shirt and cloak," he said, "so that these fine people are not tempted to laugh at me again." After he had taken the clothes, to which he was entitled under the rules of the combat, he returned the power-knife to its ceramic sheath, handling it more warily than he had done in the heat of the fight. He looked tired. One of the courtiers touched him on the arm and said coldly, "It is time to go back to the High City."

Retz bowed his head.

As he was walking toward the inn door, with the mail shirt rolled up into a heavy ball under one arm and the cloak slung loosely round his shoulders, Practal's apprentice came up and stood in his way, shouting, "Practal was the better man!"

Retz looked down at him and nodded.

"So he was."

The apprentice began to weep. "The Locust Clan will not allow you to live for this!" he said wildly.

"I don't suppose they will," said Ignace Retz.

He rubbed his neck. The courtiers hurried him out. Behind him the crowd had gone quiet. As yet, no bets were being paid out.

Mammy Vooley held a cold and disheartening court. She had been old when the Northmen brought her to the city after the War of the Two Queens. Her body was like a long ivory pole about which they had draped the faded purple gown of her predecessor. On it was supported a very small head which looked as if it had been partly scalped, partly burned, and partly starved to death in a cage suspended above the Gabelline Gate. One of her eyes was missing. She sat on an old carved wooden throne with iron wheels, in the middle of a tall whitewashed room that had five windows. Nobody knew where she had come from, not even the Northmen whose queen she had replaced. Her intelligence never diminished. At night the servants heard her singing in a thin whining voice, in some language none of them knew, as she sat among the ancient sculptures and broken machines that were the city's heritage.

Ignace Retz was ushered in to see her by the same courtiers who had led him down to the fight. They bowed to Mammy Vooley and pushed him forward, no longer bothering to disguise the contempt they felt for him. Mammy Vooley smiled at them. She extended her hand and drew Retz down close to her bald head. She stared anxiously into his face, running her fingers over his upper arms, his jaw, his scarlet crest. She examined the bruise Practal had left on his neck. As soon as she had reassured herself he had come to no harm, she pushed him away.

"Has my champion been successful in defending my

honor?" she asked. When she spoke, dim blue lights came on behind the windows, dim blue faces which seemed to repeat quietly whatever she said. "Is the man dead?"

Immediately Retz saw that he had made a mistake. He could have killed Practal, and now he wished he had. He wondered if she had been told already. He knew that whatever he said the courtiers would tell her the truth, but to avoid having to answer the question himself he threw Practal's mail shirt on the floor at her feet.

"I bring you his shirt, ma'am," he said.

She looked at him expressionlessly. A cold silence filled the room. Bubbles went up from the mouths of the faces in the windows. From behind him Retz heard someone say, "We are afraid the man is not dead, Your Majesty. Retz fought a lazy match and then hamstrung him by a crude trick. We do not understand why. His instructions were clear."

Retz laughed dangerously.

"It was not a crude trick," he said. "It was a clever one. Some day I will find a trick like that for you."

Mammy Vooley sat like a heap of sticks, her single eye directed at the ceiling.

After a moment she seemed to shrug. "It will be enough," she said remotely. "But in future you must kill them, you must always kill them. I want them killed." And her mottled hand came out again from under the folds of her robe, where tiny flakes of whitewash and damp plaster had settled like the dust in the convoluted leaves of a foreign plant. "Now give me the weapon back until the next time."

Retz massaged the side of his neck. The power-knife had left some sort of poisonous residue inside his bones, some gray vibration which made him feel leaden and nauseated. He was afraid of Mammy Vooley and even more afraid of the dead, bluish faces in the windows; he was afraid of the courtiers as they passed to and fro behind him, whispering together. But he had made so many enemies down in the Low City that tonight he must persuade her to let him keep the knife. To gain time he went down on one knee. Then he remembered something he had heard in a popular play, *The War with the Great Beetles*.

"Ma'am," he said urgently, "let me serve you further! To the south and east lie those broad wastes which threaten to swallow up Viriconium. New empires are there to be carved out, new treasures dug up! Only give me this knife, a horse, and a few men, and I will adventure there on your behalf!"

When tegeus-Cromis, desperate swordsman of *The War with the Great Beetles*, had petitioned Queen Methvet Nian in this manner, she had sent him promptly (albeit with a wan, prophetic smile) on the journey which was to lead to his defeat of the Iron Dwarf, and thence to the acquisition of immense power. Mammy Vooley only stared into space and whispered, "What are you talking about? All the empires of the world are mine already."

For a second Retz forgot his predicament, so real was his desire for that treasure which lies abandoned amid the corrupt marshes and foundering, sloth-haunted cities of the south. The clarity and anguish of his own hallucination had astonished him.

"Then, what will you give me for my services?" he demanded bitterly. "It is not as if I have failed you."

Mammy Vooley laughed.

"I will give you Osgerby Practal's mail shirt," she said, "since you have spurned the clothes I dressed you in. Now—quickly!—return me the weapon. It is not for you. It is only to defend my honor, as you well know. It must be returned after the combat."

Retz embraced Mammy Vooley's thin, oddly articulated legs and tried to put his head in her lap. He closed his eyes. He felt the courtiers pull him away. Though he kicked out vigorously, they soon stripped him of the meal-colored cloak—exclaiming in disgust at the whiteness of his thin body—and found the ceramic sheath strapped under his arm. He thought of what would happen to him when the Locust Clan caught him defenseless somewhere among the ruins at Lowth or down by the Isle of Dogs, where his mother lived. "My lady," he begged, *"lend* me the knife. I will be in need of it before dawn...." But Mammy Vooley would not speak to him. With a shriek of despair, he threw off the courtiers and pulled the knife out. Leprous white motes floated in the cold room. The bones of his arm turned to paste.

"This is all I ever got from you," he heard himself say. "And here is how I give it you back, Mammy Vooley!"

With a quick sweep of the knife he cut off the hand she had raised to dismiss him. She stared at the end of her arm, and then at Retz: her face seemed to be swimming up toward his through dark water, anxious, one-eyed, unable to understand what he had done to her.

Retz clapped his hands to his head.

He threw down the weapon, grabbed up his belongings, and—while the courtiers were still milling about in fear and confusion, dabbing numbly at their yellow cloaks where Mammy Vooley's blood had spattered them—ran moaning out of the palace. Behind him all the dim blue lips in the throne-room windows opened and closed agitatedly, like disturbed pond life.

Outside on the Proton Way he fell down quivering in the slushy snow and vomited his heart up. He lay there thinking. Two years ago I was nothing; then I became the Queen's champion and a great fighter; now they will hunt me down and I will be nothing again. He stayed there for twenty minutes. No one came after him. It was very dark. When he had calmed down and the real despair of his position had revealed itself to him, he put on Osgerby Practal's clothes and went into the Low City, where he walked about rather aimlessly until he came to a place he knew called The Bistro Californium. He sat there drinking lemon gin until the whistling began and his fear drove him out onto the streets again.

It was the last hour before dawn, and a binding frost had turned the rutted snow to ice. Retz stepped through an archway in an alley somewhere near Line Mass Quays and found himself in a deep narrow courtyard where the bulging housefronts were held apart by huge balks of timber. The bottom of this crumbling well was bitterly cold and full of a darkness unaffected by day or night; it was littered with broken pottery and other rubbish. Retz shuddered. Three sides of the courtyard had casement windows; the fourth was a blank, soot-streaked cliff studded with rusty iron bolts; high up he could see a small square of moonlit sky. For the time being he had thrown his pursuers off the scent. He had last heard them quartering the streets down by the canal. He assured himself briefly that he was alone and sat down in a doorway to wait for first light. He wrapped his woolen cloak round him.

A low whistle sounded next to his very ear. He leaped to his feet with a scream of fear and began to beat on the door of the house.

"Help!" he cried. "Murder!"

He heard quiet ironic laughter behind him in the dark.

Affiliates of the Locust Clan had driven him out of the Artists Quarter and into Lowth. There on the familiar hill he had recognized with mounting panic the squawks, shrieks, and low plaintive whistles of a dozen other factions, among them Anax-Hermax's High City Mohocks, the Feverfew Anschluss with their preternaturally drawn-out "We are all met," the Yellow Paper Men, and the Fifth of September— even the haughty mercenaries of the Blue Anemone. They had waited for him, their natural rivalries suppressed. They

had made the night sound like the inside of an aviary. Then
they had harried him to and fro across Lowth in the sleety
cold until his lungs ached, showing themselves only to keep
him moving, edging him steadily toward the High City, the
palace: and Mammy Vooley. He believed they would not
attack him in a private house, or in daylight, if he could
survive until then.

"Help!" he shouted. "Please, help!"

Suddenly one of the casements above him flew open and
a head appeared, cocked alertly to one side. Retz waved
his arms. "Murder!" The window slammed shut again. He
moaned and battered harder at the door while behind him
the piercing whistles of the Yellow Paper Men filled the
courtyard. When he looked up, the timber balks were
swarming with figures silhouetted against the sky. They
wanted him out of the yard and into the city again. Someone
plucked at his shoulder, whispering. When he struck out,
whoever was there cut him lightly across the back of the
hand. A moment later the door opened and he fell through
it into a dimly lit hall where an old man in a deep blue robe
waited for him with a candle.

At the top of some stairs behind the heavy baize curtain
at the end of the hall there was a large room with stone
floor and plastered white walls, kept above the freezing
point by a pan of glowing charcoal. It was furnished with
heavy wooden chairs, a sideboard of a great age, and a
lectern in the shape of an eagle whose outspread wings
supported an old book. Along one wall hung a tapestry,
ragged and out of keeping with the rest of the room, which
was that of an abbot, a judge, or a retired soldier. The old
man made Retz sit in one of the chairs and held the candle
up so that he could examine Retz's scarlet crest, which he
had evidently mistaken for the result of a head wound.

After a moment he sighed impatiently.

"Just so," he said.

"Sir," said Retz, squinting up at him, "are you a doctor?" And, "Sir, you are holding the candle so that I cannot see you."

This was not quite true. If he moved his head he could make out an emaciated yellow face, long and intelligent-looking, the thin skin stretched over the bones like waxed paper over a lamp.

"So I am," said the old man. "Are you hungry?" Without waiting for an answer, he went to the window and looked out. "Well, you have outwitted the other wolves and will live another day. Wait here." And he left the room.

Retz passed his hands wearily over his eyes. His nausea abated, the sweat dried in the hollow of his back, the whistles of the Yellow Paper Men moved off east toward the canal and eventually died away. After a few minutes he got up and warmed himself over the charcoal pan, spreading his fingers over it, then rubbing the palms of his hands together mechanically while he stared at the lectern in the middle of the room. It was made of good steel, and he wondered how much it might fetch in the pawn shops of the Margarethestrasse. His breath steamed in the cold air. Who was the old man? His furniture was expensive. When he comes back, Retz thought, I will ask him for his protection. Perhaps he will give me the eagle so that I can buy a horse and leave the city. An old man like him could easily afford that. Retz examined the porcelain plates on the sideboard. He stared at the tapestry. Large parts of it were so decayed he could not understand what they were meant to show; but in one corner he could make out a hill and the steep path which wound up it between stones and the roots of old trees. It made him feel uncomfortable and lonely.

When the old man returned he was carrying a tray with a pie and some bread on it. Two or three cats followed him into the room, looking up at him expectantly in the brown, wavering light of the candle. He found Retz in front of the tapestry.

"Come away from there!" he said sharply.

"Sir," said Retz, bowing low, "you saved my life. Tell me how I can serve you."

"I would not want a murderer for a servant," replied the old man.

Retz bit his underlip angrily. He turned his back, sat down, and began to stuff bread into his mouth. "If you lived out there you would act like me!" he said indistinctly. "What else is there?"

"I have lived in this city for more years than I can remember," said the old man. "I have murdered no one."

At this there was a longish silence. The old man sat with his chin on his chest and appeared lost in thought. The charcoal pan ticked as it cooled; a draft caught the tapestry so that it billowed like a torn net curtain in the Boulevard Aussman; the cats scratched about furtively in the shadows behind the chairs. Ignace Retz ate, drank, wiped his mouth; he ate more and wiped his mouth again. When he was sure the old man wasn't watching him, he boldly appraised the steel eagle. Once, on the pretext of going to the window, he even got up and touched it.

"What horror we are all faced with daily!" exclaimed the old man suddenly.

He sighed.

"I have heard the café philosophers say: 'The world is so old that the substance of reality no longer knows quite what it ought to be. The original template is lost. History repeats over and again this one city and a few frightful events—not rigidly, but in a shadowy, tentative fashion, as if it understands nothing else but would like to learn.'"

"The world is the world," said Ignace Retz. "Whatever they say."

"Look at the tapestry," said the old man.

Retz looked. The design he had made out earlier, with its mountain path and stunted yew trees, was more extensive than he had thought. In it a bald man was depicted trudging up the path. Above him in the air hung a large bird. Beyond that, more mountains and valleys went away to the horizon. No stitching could be seen. The whole was worked very carefully and realistically, so that Retz felt that he was looking through a window. The man on the path had skin of a yellowish color, and his cloak was blue. He leaned on his staff as if he was out of breath. Without warning he turned round and stared out of the tapestry at Retz. As he did so the tapestry rippled in a cold draft, giving off a damp smell, and the whole scene vanished.

Retz began to tremble. In the distance he heard the old man say, "There is no need to be frightened."

"It is alive," Retz whispered. "Mammy Vooley—" But before he could say what he meant, another scene had presented itself.

It was dawn in Viriconium. The sky was a bowl of cloud with a litharge stain at its edge. Rain fell on the Proton Way where, supported by a hundred pillars of black stone, it spiraled up toward the palace. Halfway along this bleak ancient sweep of road two or three figures in glowing scarlet armor stood watching a man fight with a vulture made of metal. The man's face was terribly cut; blood and rain made a dark mantle on his shoulders as he knelt there on the road. But he was winning. Soon he rose tiredly to his feet and threw the bird down in front of the watchers, who turned away and would not acknowledge him. He stared out of the tapestry. His cheeks hung open where the bird had pecked him; he was old and gray-haired, and his eyes were full of regret. His lips moved and he disappeared.

"It was me!" cried Ignace Retz. "Was it me?"

"There have been many Viriconiums," said the old man. "Watch the tapestry."

Two men with rusty swords stumbled across a high moor. A long way behind them came a dwarf wearing mechanical iron stilts. His head was laid open with a wound. They waited for him to catch up, but he fell behind again almost immediately. He blundered into a rowan tree and went off in the wrong direction. One of the men, who looked like Ignace Retz, had a dead bird swinging from his belt. He stared dispiritedly out of the tapestry at the real Retz, took the bird in one hand, and raised it high in the air by its neck. As he made this gesture the dwarf passed in front of him, his stilts leaking unhealthy white gasses. They forded a stream together, and all three of them vanished into the distance where a city waited on a hill.

After that, men fought one another in the shadow of a cliff, while above them on the eroded skyline patrolled huge iridescent beetles. A fever-stricken explorer with despairing eyes sat in a cart and allowed himself to be pulled along slowly by an animal like a tall white sloth until they came to the edge of a pool in a flooded city. Lizards circled endlessly a pile of corpses in the desert.

Eventually Retz grew used to seeing himself at the center of these events, although he was sometimes surprised by the way he looked. But the last scene was too much for him.

He seemed to be looking through a tall, arched window, around the stone mullions of which twined the stems of an ornamental rose. The thorns and flowers of the rose framed a room where curtains of silver light drifted like rain between enigmatic columns. The floor of the room was made of cinnabar crystal and in the center of it had been set a simple throne. Standing by the throne, two albino lions couchant at her feet, was a slender woman in a velvet gown. Her eyes were a deep, sympathetic violet color, her hair the russet of autumn leaves. On her long fingers she wore ten identical rings, and before her stood a knight whose glowing scarlet armor was partly covered by a black and silver cloak. His head was bowed. His hands were white. At his side he wore a steel sword.

Retz heard the woman say clearly, "I give you these things, Lord tegeus-Cromis, because I trust you. I would even give you a power-knife if I had one. Go to the south and win great treasure for us all."

Out of the tapestry drifted the scent of roses on a warm evening. There was the gentle sound of falling water, and somewhere a single line of melody repeated over and over again on a stringed instrument. The knight in the scarlet armor took his queen's hand and kissed it. He turned to look out of the window and wave as if someone he knew was passing. His black hair was parted in the middle to frame the transfigured face of Ignace Retz. Behind him the queen was smiling. The whole scene vanished, leaving a smell of damp, and all that could be seen through the rents in the cloth was the plaster on the wall.

Ignace Retz rubbed his eyes furiously. He jumped up, pulled the old man out of his chair, clutched him by the upper arm, and dragged him up to the tapestry.

"Those last things!" he demanded. "Have they really happened?"

"All queens are not Mammy Vooley," said the old man, as if he had won an argument. "All knights are not Ignace Retz. They have happened, or will."

"Make it show me again."

"I cannot. I am a caretaker. I cannot compel."

Retz pushed him away with such violence that he fell against the sideboard and knocked the tray off it. The cats ran excitedly about, picking up pieces of food in their mouths.

"I must not believe this!" cried Retz. He pulled the tapestry off the wall and examined it intently, as if he hoped to see himself moving there. When it remained mere cloth he threw it on the floor and kicked at it. "How could I live my life if I believed this?" he asked himself. He turned back to the old man, took him by the shoulders, and shook him. "What did you want to show me this for? How can I be content with this ghastly city now?"

"You need not live as you do," said the old man. "We make the world we live in."

Retz threw him aside. He hit his head on the sideboard, gave a curious angry groan, and was still. He did not seem to be dead. For some minutes Retz lurched distractedly to and fro between the window and the wall where the tapestry had been, repeating, "How can I live? How can I live!" Then he rushed over to the lectern and tried to wrench the steel eagle off it. It would be daylight by now, out in the city; they would be coughing and warming their hands by the naphtha flares in the Tinmarket. He would have a few hours in which to sell the bird, get a horse and a knife, and leave before the bravos began hunting him again. He would go out of the Haunted Gate on his horse, and go south, and never see the place again.

The bird moved. At first he thought it was simply coming loose from the plinth of black wood on which it was set. Then he felt a sharp pain in the palm of his left hand, and when he looked down the thing was alive and struggling powerfully in his grip. It cocked its head, stared up at him out of a cold, violent eye. It got one wing free, then the other, and redoubled its efforts. He managed to hold on to it for a second or two longer, then, crying out in revulsion and panic, he let go and staggered back, shaking his lacerated hands. He fell over something on the floor and found himself staring into the old man's stunned china-blue eyes.

"Get out of my house!" shouted the old man. "I've had enough of you!"

The bird meanwhile rose triumphantly into the air and flapped round the room, battering its wings against the walls and shrieking, while coppery reflections flared off its plumage and the cats crouched terrified underneath the furniture.

"Help me!" appealed Retz. "The eagle is alive!" But the old man, lying on the floor as if paralyzed, set his lips and would only answer, "You have brought it on yourself."

Retz stood up and tried to cross the room to the door at the head of the stairs. The bird, which had been obsessively attacking its own shadow on the wall, promptly fastened itself over his face, striking at his eyes and tearing with its talons at his neck and upper chest. He screamed. He pulled it off him and dashed it against the base of the wall, where it fluttered about in a disoriented fashion for a moment before making off after one of the cats. Retz watched it, appalled, then clapped his hands to his bleeding face and blundered out of the room, down the narrow staircase, and out into the courtyard again. He slammed the door behind him.

It was still dark.

Sitting on the doorstep, Retz felt his neck cautiously to determine the extent of his injuries. He shuddered. They were not shallow. Above him he could still hear the trapped bird shrieking and beating its wings. If it escaped it would find him. As soon as he had stopped bleeding, he backed shakily away across the courtyard and passed through the arch into a place he did not know.

He was on a wide, open avenue flanked by ruined buildings and heaps of rubble. Meaningless trenches had been dug across it here and there, and desultory fires burned on every side. Dust covered the broken chestnut trees and uprooted railings. Although there was no sign at all of dawn, the sky somehow managed to throw a curious blue light over everything. Behind him the walled courtyard now stood on its own like a kind of blank rectangular tower. He thought he was still looking at the old man's tapestry; he thought there might have been some sort of war in the night with Mammy Vooley's devastating weapons; he didn't know what to think. He started to walk nervously in the direction of the canal, then run. He ran for a long time but could not find it. Acres of shattered roof tiles made a musical scraping sound under his feet. If he looked back he could still see the tower; but it got smaller and smaller, and in the end he forgot where to look for it.

All through that long night he had no idea where he was, but he felt as if he must be on a high plateau, windy and covered completely with the dust and rubble of this unfamiliar city. The wind stung the wounds the bird had given him. The dust pattered and rained against the fallen walls. Once he heard some kind of music coming from a distant house—the febrile beating of a large flat drum, the reedy, fitful whine of something like a clarinet—but when he approached the place it was silent again, and he became frightened.

Later a human voice from the ruins quite near him made a long drawn out *ou lou lou lou,* and was answered immediately from far off by a howl like a dog's. He fled from it between the long mounds of rubble, and for a while hid in the gutted shell of a cathedrallike building. After he had been there for about an hour, several indistinct figures appeared outside and began to dig silently and energetically in the road. Suddenly, though, they were disturbed; they all looked up together at something Retz couldn't see, and ran off with their spades. While this was going on he heard feet scraping around him in the bluish dark. There was a deep sigh. *Ou lou lou* sounded, shockingly close, and he was alone again. They had examined him, whoever they were, and found him of no interest.

Toward dawn he left the building to look at the trench they had dug in the road. It was shallow, abortive, already filling up with gray sand. About a mile away he found a dead man, hidden by a corner of masonry that stood a little over waist high.

Retz knelt down and studied him curiously.

He lay as if he had fallen heavily while running away from someone, his limbs all askew and one arm evidently broken. He was heavily built, dressed in a loose white shirt and black moleskin trousers tied up below the knees with red string. He had on a fish-head mask, a thing like a salmon with blubbery lips, lugubrious popping eyes, and a crest of stiff spines, worn in such a way that if he had been standing upright the fish would have been staring glassily into the sky. Green ribbons were tied round his upper arms to flutter and rustle in the wind. Beside him where he had dropped it lay a power-knife from which there rose, as it burned its way into the rubble, a steady stream of poisonous yellow motes.

They had taken off his boots. His naked white feet were decorated with blue tattoos which went this way and that like veins.

Retz stared thoughtfully down at him. He climbed onto the wall and looked carefully both ways along the empty road. Whatever place the old man and the bird had consigned him to, it would have its Mammy Vooley. He would have to fit in. It was in his nature. Ten minutes later he emerged from behind the wall dressed in the dead man's clothes. They were too large, and he had some trouble with the fish head, which stank inside, but he had tied on the red string and the ribbons, and he had the knife. By the time he finished all this dawn had come at last, a lid of brownish cloud tilted back at its eastern rim on streaks of yellow and emerald green, revealing a steep hill he had not previously seen. It was topped with towers, old fortifications, and the copper domes of ancient observatories. Retz set off in the direction the trench-diggers had taken. "Shroggs Royd" announced the plaques at the corners of the demolished streets: "Ouled Nail." Then: "Rue Sepile."

That afternoon there was a dry storm. Particles of dust flew about under a leaden sky.

Events Witnessed From a City

IN THE COMPANY OF RATS, Dissolution Kahn and Choplogic
the dwarf sat beneath the dome of the derelict observatory
at Alves, discussing the peculiarities of time and the uncertain nature of events.

"Further," whispered the dwarf, revealing briefly his decaying teeth as if they offered a useful metaphysical clue,
"I would mistrust people who do things—I would laugh
circumspectly at their reason for doing them—contingency,
after all, is contingency."

Vira Co, the city in the waste, spread itself below them
in the wet equivocal afternoon light like excavations interrupted in a sunken garden. They regarded with some amuse-
ment the watchfulness of the footmen along the outer walls.
The dwarf left his position at the embrasure and began to
strut about.

"If the human race continues to breed, it will continue—
an act of extreme bad taste. On the other hand, what an
extraordinary gesture, to free ourselves from our own bi-
ology. The refusal to give birth is a splendid beginning."

He stalked through the gloom between the old telescopes,
his hand on his weapon.

"It is a Miltonic statement of intent, I agree," said Dissolution Kahn. He had in his hands a clockwork orrery,
whose jeweled planets he watched eagerly through a full
rotation. He gestured at the star charts peeling off the walls.

"It must surely provoke some reaction." He took out his pewter snuffbox. "It can hardly be ignored in fact." He sneezed.

"That possibility must be allowed for," chuckled the dwarf. Quick as a lizard, he drew his little sword and flung himself across the floor. He impaled one rat, and then another. They struggled; how they squealed!

Choplogic snickered. His friend joined in. Their raucous laughter fled from the embrasures and out over the city.

After four millennia motionless on its axis, the Earth had begun to turn again.

From a semiorganic tower three miles inside the dark hemisphere, tegeus-Cromis the poet watched the twilight crawl toward him, a few laborious inches every twenty-four hours: a strange new movement reflected in events which his instruments detected: novel forms, new seasons, fresh miscegenations.

Inbred Cromis (son of his sister, dark-haired and skeletal in the sad wash of light) watched his indicators creep across their meters, witnessing the slow birth-trauma of the sun as it was squeezed up over the rim of the world. Three miles separated him from the crepuscular zone—three miles and a century. Often he would smile, thin lips limned with blue phosphorescence as he thought about the hundred-year dawn.

He had a visitor.

She came out of the complicated landforms of the twilight sector, hugging the contours, moving fast but carefully. She glittered like an armored fish, her pink roan hair blown back by strong winds. The organic tower hummed. The thin hands of tegeus-Cromis skittered like rats across his instrument panel. Her face leaped toward him. Her lips, he saw, were bloodless. The rats scuttled, and she receded. *A silver leash trailed from her left hand.*

Behind her stepped a crane fly half as tall as the tower,

its slow stilted legs and slim trembling abdomen chased
with colored arabesques and sphenograms. Eyes like clus-
ters of ruby lasers. It moved hesitantly. Huge bats orbited
its pointed mask like shredded black cloaks, their sonar
emissions interfering with cerise displays in the instrument
room, their indistinct telepathies flickering to him in banks
of colored light.

"Why should I let you in?" he asked when she had reached
the base of the tower. His voice hooted through the darkness,
carefully distorted to sound like the wind.

"Come to Vira Co," she answered. She stirred the spoiled
earth with her foot, making singular diagrams.

The crane fly clicked. "Come to the city," it said.

The woman began to fade, losing substance until his
screens would register nothing. He attempted to follow her
with his fingers, throwing switches, increasing the gain of
the sensors. She vanished anyway; although the afterimage
of the insect remained for some time, fluorescing.

Out along the city wall, proctors kept the view.

Beyond the twilight sector, from the millennial darkness
in the west, the towers of the poets moaned and hooted,
exchanging data across the damaged continent, huge voices
modulating with the wind, at times immensely distant, at
others close to hand. New shapes moved cautiously in the
twilight, gasping for breath, or trying to decide what breath
was.

Their dark cloaks flapping uneasily, the watchers toured
their battlements. They murmured in low voices. They
hooded their faces when the guard was changed and hurried
away on urgent errands. They were beset by a sense of
immanence:

". . . the darkness moving to fresh rhythms!"

"Confirmation expected almost immediately . . ."

". . . fear death from the air . . ."

"We anticipate a visit."

Bats overflew the city, to haunt its higher tenements in Montrouge and Cheminor. None were sighted in or around the observatory at Alves.

"Things are. Things happen. Do nothing," whispered the proctors.

"It may be a little late for that."

Indecisive Cromis assumed his tower had dreamed it all. He tapped his fingers gently against its flesh. He rendered it unconscious and sat silently in the gloom. Its tissues remained healthy and sane. It was not senile. He had tended it for seven centuries. (It had, too, served his father well.)

He took up a small ornate syringe, the property of an ancestor of his before the world had ceased to turn, wrapped a cloak of deceptive color about his thin body, and made his way down arteries of pale, unsteady light to the entrance of the brain chamber, a smooth gray tumor in the meat of a corridor wall.

He shook his head. He swabbed his inner elbow and took a small amount of veinal blood. This he injected into the tumor. After a moment the ancient defences identified him and the lips of a sphincter formed. He pushed them apart and entered.

The brain moaned drowsily at him.

"You had a dream."

The brain reminded him that it could not dream.

He refilled his baroque spike, stabbed.

"Relate me your dream."

The brain reminded him that it could not dream.

He stroked its smoother parts.

"Relate the dream."

Nothing was solved.

•   •   •

"It is the sin of *superbia*," said Choplogic the dwarf, spitting his rats lengthwise so as to cook them to a nicety. "It is the sin of desiring an existence separate from one's own dreary instincts—a simultaneous sin against Darwin and God."

He made a small fire of the remaining astrological maps and implements.

"Celibacy," he said. "It is the last freedom. It is the ultimate art."

"More food, too." Dissolution Kahn rubbed his beard. "Look here, I seem to have broken this." And indeed the golden orrery no longer performed its mechanical cycles. He took out his knife and investigated the clockwork with its point. At a loss, he prized the rubies from the outer planets and threw them on the floor.

"It worked beautifully before."

Later, grease dripping down his chin, Choplogic returned to the western embrasure. Out there in the dark zone, the organic towers trumpeted across the wastes, measurements and warnings. He could make out no words, so he returned to his study of the city.

"What a sense of liberty is gained by the performance of one symbolic act on the grand scale," he mused. He spat out some bones.

The Kahn, polishing the brass spikes on his black leather gloves, nodded. "The proctors are steadily deserting their posts," he said. "Few remain. We would seem to have won freedom from secular authority as well as from supernal." He laughed. "If you do not breed, and if you do not care whether you live or die, what sanction have they left, after all?"

They slept. When they woke they caught and ate more rats. The long afternoon wore on.

• • •

Down in Luthos Plaza and Replica Square, in the cellars of the Blue Metal Discovery and all about the base of the cobbled hill at Alves, the citizens held celebration of certain salient points in the overlong history of the Afternoon Cultures: Bruton's destruction of the machine in Shaft Ten; the global rationalizations of Crispin Wendover and the Ministry of Intent; the final braking of the Earth's rotation by Rotgob Mungo in the so-called "year of the little decision."

Gerard Paucemanly addressed a gathering by electric megaphone, wearing his nicest silver lamé. He drank half a pint of amyl nitrate. "Strip the bark off a green tree today!" he cried. "Cheerio!" He fell over.

"Burn it off and lay concrete!" his friends applauded.

Lady Angina Seng, standing straddle-legged at the summit of her funeral pyre, sang a new song: "I don't need anything here/I don't have any luggage to carry except this one dislike." She injected herself with fifty milligrams of Tryptizone directly into the left ventricle of her heart. Her lover wandered off.

All the withered fortune-tellers of Margery Fry Court went out slowly, like spotlights, swapping gossip from more delicate days: "Headlights waltzing on the tennis courts!" "Could this be a limbo?" Nothing was saved but their tea leaves and their tiny linen handkerchiefs smelling of parma violets.

"Choose your personal backdrop," urged the undertakers' men. "If they look to the east they may not see your flames; to the west your smoke may be invisible."

Apostate proctors, committing the sin of despair, threaded the gaudy backstreets in search of a sensation or two.

Dr. Grishkin, the man with the window in his stomach, sawed off his own right arm.

Clowns burst from the arena.

Out in the waste, the tower of tegeus-Cromis ran checking-sequences, browsing the megacycles. Receptors charted exchanges between this or that blind animal. Plumbed the burrows of lizards. The amplifier stacks hummed; the dark hemisphere of Earth groaned and hooted.

Cromis bared his inner elbow, fed himself on glucose while the indicators crept. He had lost his pleasure in the long dawn. He could think only of the illusory woman. Her face hung over him when he slept: smiles and grimaces were on it, in no logical order; she whispered and bit her own lips.

He took the luminous arteries to the brain-chamber.

"Relate me a list of the Old Instincts."

In search of relief he ran a sterile tube from an incision in his wrist to a sphincter in the chamber wall. The brain-room screens, possessed by blood-cell images of fish, hallucinated a jeweled cup. He was losing his ascendancy.

Later, the tower trembled beneath him.

He clutched at his syringe. He was at a loss. He stumbled through the arteries of his home and discovered chambers and oubliettes he had never seen before. The woman was there, urging him toward her. The tower shuddered. He dropped his cloak.

Finally, from the undersea gloaming of the instrument room, he called for help from the other towers. The dark side snickered at him ("Big lizard—little lizard—a hungry bat"), and the amplifiers failed to respond. And when the inconceivable lurching began, he could not tell whether it was a function of the tower or of the Earth. Instruments showed him an image of the world swaying and staggering. They showed him the twilight sector, growing closer.

Events witnessed on the city wall:

Two proctors remained there. The wind cut them as they stared into the west.

"The darkness is moving to fresh rhythms," murmured Choplogic the dwarf.

Black smoke rose from the pyres in the city beneath. Whirled away by strong winds, it carried the bats before it like a million ragged cloaks.

Reluctantly he abandoned his vantage point at the window.

He studied the interior of the observatory for a moment, showing his filthy teeth.

He placed the hilt of his little sword carefully against the ribcage of the dead Kahn. It shone in the dim brown light of the afternoon. He pushed himself onto its point, groaning quietly. The observatory walls faded momentarily. He clutched his stomach.

"Admire the death-rate solution," he whispered, staring into the eyes of his dead friend as if they offered some cautious metaphysical clue.

Then he dragged himself back to the embrasure to smile at the great gray fleshy towers of the dark side, as, hooting and lowing across the cryptic landscape beyond Vira Co, they advanced on the city, dreaming as they came.

The Luck in the Head

UROCONIUM, ARDWICK CROME said, was for all its beauty an indifferent city. Its people loved the arena; they were burning or quartering somebody every night for political or religious crimes. They hadn't much time for anything else. From where he lived, at the top of a tenement on the outskirts of Montrouge, you could often see the fireworks in the dark, or hear the shouts on the wind.

He had two rooms. In one of them was an iron-frame bed with a few blankets on it, pushed up against a washstand he rarely used. Generally he ate his meals cold, though he had once tried to cook an egg by lighting a newspaper under it. He had a chair, and a tall white ewer with a picture of the courtyard of an inn on it. The other room, a small northlight studio once occupied—so tradition in the Artists Quarter had it—by Kristodulos Fleece the painter, he kept shut. It had some of his books in it, also the clothes in which he had first come to Uroconium and which he had thought then were fashionable.

He was not a well-known poet, although he had his following.

Every morning he would write for perhaps two hours, first restricting himself to the bed by means of three broad leather straps which his father had given him and which he

fastened himself, at the ankles, the hips, and finally across
his chest. The sense of unfair confinement or punishment
induced by this, he found, helped him to think.

Sometimes he called out or struggled; often he lay quite
inert and looked dumbly up at the ceiling. He had been born
in those vast dull plowlands which roll east from Soubridge
into the Midland Levels like a chocolate-colored sea, and
his most consistent work came from the attempt to retrieve
and order the customs and events of his childhood there;
the burial of the "Holly Man" on Plow Monday, the sound
of the hard black lupine seeds popping and tapping against
the window in August while his mother sang quietly in the
kitchen the ancient carols of the Oei'l Voirrey. He remembered the meadows and reeds beside the Yser Canal, the
fishes that moved within it. When his straps chafed, the old
bridges were in front of him, made of warm red brick and
curved protectively over their own image in the water!

Thus Crome lived in Uroconium, remembering, working, publishing. He sometimes spent an evening in the Bistro
Californium or the Luitpold Café. Several of the Luitpold
critics (notably Barzelletta Angst, who in *L'Espace Cromien*
ignored entirely the conventional chronology—expressed
in the idea of "recherché"—of Crome's long poem *Bream
Into Man*) tried to represent his work as a series of narra-
tiveless images, glued together only by his artistic persona.
Crome refuted them in a pamphlet. He was content.

Despite his sedentary habits, he was a sound sleeper.
But before it blows at night over the pointed roofs of Montrouge, the southwest wind must first pass between the abandoned towers of the Old City, as silent as burned logs, full
of birds, scraps of machinery, and broken-up philosophies;
and Crome had hardly been there three years when he began
to have a dream in which he was watching the ceremony
called the "Luck in the Head."

For its proper performance this ceremony requires the

construction of a seashore, between the low- and high-tide marks at the Eve of Assumption, of two fences or "hedges." These are made by weaving osiers—usually cut at dawn on the same day—through split hawthorn uprights upon which the foliage has been left. The men of the town stand at one end of the corridor thus formed, the women, their thumbs tied together behind their backs, at the other. At a signal the men release between the hedges a lamb decorated with medallions, paper ribbons and strips of rag. The women race after, catch it, and scramble to keep it from one another, the winner being the one who can seize the back of the animal's neck with her teeth. In Dunham Massey, Lymm, and Iron Chine, the lamb is paraded for three days on a pole before being made into pies; and it is good luck to obtain the pie made from the head.

In his dream Crome found himself standing on some sand dunes, looking out over the wastes of marram grass at the osier-fences and the tide. The women, with their small heads and long gray garments, stood breathing heavily like horses, or walked nervously in circles avoiding one another's eyes as they tested with surreptitious tugs the red cord which bound their thumbs. Crome could see no one there he knew. Somebody said, "A hundred eggs and a calf's tail," and laughed. Ribbons fluttered in the cold air: they had introduced the lamb. It stood quite still until the women, who had been lined up and settled down after a certain amount of jostling, rushed at it. Their shrieks rose up like those of herring gulls, and a fine rain came in from the sea.

"They're killing one another!" Crome heard himself say.

Without any warning, one of them burst out of the melee with the lamb in her teeth. She ran up the dunes with a floundering, splay-footed gait and dropped it at his feet. He stared down at it.

"It's not mine," he said. But everyone else had walked away.

He woke up listening to the wind and staring at the washstand, got out of bed, and walked round the room to quiet himself down. Fireworks, greenish and queasy with the hour of the night, lit up the air intermittently above the distant arena. Some of this illumination, entering through the skylight, fell as a pale wash on his thin arms and legs, fixing them in attitudes of despair.

If he went to sleep again he often found, in a second lobe or episode of the dream, that he had already accepted the dead lamb and was himself running with it at a steady, premeditated trot down the landward side of the dunes toward the town. (This he recognized by its slate roofs as Lowick, a place he had once visited in childhood. In its streets some men made tiny by distance were banging on doors with sticks, as they had done then. He remembered very clearly the piece of singed sheepskin they had been making people smell.) Empty ground stretched away on either side of him under a motionless sky; everything—the clumps of thistles, the frieze of small thorn trees deformed by the wind, the sky itself—had a brownish cast, as if seen through an atmosphere of tars. He could hear the woman behind him to begin with, but soon he was left alone. In the end Lowick vanished too, though he began to run as quickly as he could, and left him in a mist or smoke through which a bright light struck, only to be diffused immediately.

By then the lamb had become something that produced a thick buzzing noise, a vibration which percolated up the bones of his arm and into his shoulders, then into the right side of his neck and face where it reduced the muscles to water; it made him feel nauseated, weak, and deeply afraid. Whatever it was, he couldn't shake it off his hand.

Clearly—in that city and at that age of the world—it would have been safer for Crome to look inside himself for the source of this dream. Instead, after he had waked one day with the early light coming through the shutters like sour milk and a vague rheumatic ache in his neck, he went out into Uroconium to pursue it. He was sure he would recognize the woman if he saw her—or the lamb.

She was not in the Bistro Californium when he went there by way of the Via Varese, or in Mecklenburgh Square. He looked for her in Proton Alley, where the beggars gaze back at you emptily and the pavement artists offer to draw for you, in that curious mixture of powdered chalk and condensed milk they favor, pictures of the Lamia without clothes or without skin, with fewer limbs or organs than normal, or more. They couldn't draw the woman he wanted. On the Unter-Main-Kai (it was eight in the morning and the naphtha flares had grown smoky and dim) a boy spun and tottered among the crowds from the arena, declaiming in a language no one knew. He uncovered his cropped head, raised his bony face to the sky. He croaked and stuck long thorns in his own throat: at this the women rushed up to him and thrust upon him cakes, cosmetic emeralds, coins. Crome studied their faces: nothing. In the Luitpold Café he found Ansel Verdigris and some others eating gooseberries steeped in gin.

"I am cold and sick," said Verdigris, clutching Crome's hand.

He spooned up a few more gooseberries and then, letting the spoon fall back into the dish with a clatter, rested his head on the tablecloth beside it. From this position he was forced to stare up sideways at Crome and talk with one side of his mouth. The skin beneath his eyes had the shine of wet pipe clay; his coxcomb of reddish-yellow hair hung damp and awry; the electric light, falling oblique and bluish across his white triangular face, lent it an expression of astonishment.

"My brain is poisoned with disease, Crome," he said, "and my heart is foul. We'll go, we two, into the hills, and throw snow at one another."

He looked round with contempt at his friends, Gunther

Verlac and the Baron de V——, who grinned sheepishly
back.

"Look at them!" he said. "Crome, we're the only human
beings here. We'll renew our purity! We'll dance and play
on the lips of the icy gorges!"

"It's the wrong season for snow," said Crome.

"Well, then," Verdigris whispered, "let's go where the
old machines leak and flicker and you can hear the calls of
the madmen from the asylum up at Wergs. Listen—"

"No!" said Crome. He wrenched his hand away.

"Listen, proctors are out after me from Cheminor to
Mynned! Lend me some money, Crome, I'm sick of my
crimes. Last night they shadowed me along the cinder paths
among the poplar trees by the isolation hospital."

He laughed and began to eat gooseberries as fast as he
could.

"The dead remember only the streets, never the numbers
of the houses!"

Verdigris lived with his widowed mother, a woman of
some means and education who called herself Madame "L",
in Delpine Square. She was in a condition of perpetual
tender anxiety about his health and he about hers. They lay
ill with shallow fevers and deep cafards, in rooms with
connecting doors so that they could keep up each other's
spirits in the wearisome sleepless afternoons. When they
felt a little better they would have themselves pushed side
by side in wheelchairs through the gardens of the Haadenbosk, from gallery to museum, from this salon to that,
making gay little jokes as they went. Once a month Verdigris
would leave her and spend all night at the arena with some
prostitute, fall unconscious in the Luitpold or the Californium, and wake up distraught a few hours later in his own
bed. His greatest fear was that he would catch syphilis.
Crome looked down at him.

"You've never been to Cheminor, Verdigris," he said.
"Neither of us have."

Verdigris stared at the tablecloth. Suddenly he stuffed it into his mouth—his empty dish fell onto the floor where it rolled about for a moment, faster and faster, and was smashed—only to throw back his head and pull it out again, inch by inch, like a medium pulling out ectoplasm in Margery Fry Court.

"You won't be so pleased with yourself," he said, "when you've read this."

And he gave Crome a sheet of thick green paper, folded three times, on which someone had written:

"A man may have many kinds of dreams. There are dreams he wishes to continue and others he does not. At one hour of the night men may have dreams in which everything is veiled in violet; at others, unpalatable truths may be conveyed. If a *certain man* wants certain dreams he may be having to cease, he will wait by the Aqualate Pond at night, and speak to whomever he finds there."

"This means nothing to me," lied Crome. "Where did you get it?"

"A woman thrust it into my hand two days ago as I came down the Ghibbeline Stair. She spoke your name, or one like it. I saw nothing."

Crome stared at the sheet of paper in his hand. Leaving the Luitpold Café a few minutes later, he heard someone say: "In Aachen, by the Haunted Gate—do you remember?—a woman on the pavement stuffing cakes into her mouth? Sugar cakes into her mouth?"

That night, as Crome made his way reluctantly toward the Aqualate Pond, the moonlight rose like a lemon-yellow tide over the blackened towers and empty cat-infested palaces of the city. In the Artists Quarter the violin and cor anglais pronounced their fitful whine, while from the distant arena—from twenty-five thousand faces underlit by the flames of the auto-da-fé—issued an interminable whisper of laughter.

It was the anniversary of the liberation of Uroconium from the Analeptic Kings.

Householders lined the steep hill up at Alves. Great velvet banners, stitched with black crosses on a red and white ground, hung down from the balconies above their naked heads. Their eyes were patiently fixed on the cracked copper dome of the observatory at its summit. (There, as the text sometimes called "The Earl of Rone" remembers, the Kings handed over to Mammy Vooley and her fighters their weapons of appalling power; there they were made to bend the knee.) A single bell rang out, then stopped. . . . A hundred children carrying candles swept silently down toward them and were gone! Others came behind, shuffling to the rhythms of the "Ou lou lou," that ancient song. In the middle of it all, the night and the banners and the lights, swaying precariously to and fro fifteen feet above the procession like a doll nailed on a gilded chair, came Mammy Vooley herself.

Sometimes as it blows across the Great Brown Waste in summer, the wind will uncover a bit of petrified wood. What oak or mountain ash this wood has come from, alive immeasurably long ago, what secret treaties were made beneath it during the Afternoon of the world only to be broken by the Evening, we do not know. We will never know. It is a kind of wood full of contradictory grains and lines: studded with functionless knots: hard.

Mammy Vooley's head had the shape and the shiny gray look of wood like that. It was provided with one good eye, as if at some time it had grown round a glass marble streaked with milky blue. She bobbed it stiffly right and left to the crowds who stood to watch her approach, knelt as she passed, and stood up again behind her. Her bearers grunted patiently under the weight of the pole that bore her up. As they brought her slowly closer it could be seen that her dress— so curved between her bony, strangely articulated knees that dead leaves, lumps of plaster, and crusts of wholemeal bread had gathered in her lap—was russet-orange, and that she wore askew on the top of her head a hank of faded purple hair, wispy and fine like a very old woman's. Mammy Vooley, celebrating with black banners and young women chanting; Mammy Vooley, Queen of Uroconium, Moderator of the city, as silent as a log of wood.

Crome got up on tiptoe to watch. He had never seen her before. As she drew level with him she seemed to float in the air, her shadow projected on a cloud of candle-smoke by the lemon yellow moon. That afternoon, for the ceremony, in her salle or retiring room (where at night she might be heard singing to herself in different voices), they had painted on her face another one—approximate, like a doll's, with pink cheeks. All round Crome's feet the householders of Alves knelt in the gutter. He stared at them. Mammy Volley caught him standing.

She waved down at her bearers.

"Stop!" she whispered.

"I bless all my subjects," she told the kneeling crowd. "Even this one."

And she allowed her head to fall exhaustedly to one side.

In a moment she had passed by. The remains of the procession followed her, trailing its smell of burned wick and sweating feet, and with a dying cry in the distance vanished round a corner toward Montrouge. (Young men and women fought for the privilege of carrying the Queen. As the new bearers tried to take it from the old ones, Mammy Vooley's pole swung backward and forward in uncontrollable arcs, so that she flopped about in her chair at the top of it like the head of a mop. Wrestling silently, the small figures carried her away.) In the streets below Alves there was a sense of relief; smiling and chatting and remarking how well the Mammy had looked that day, the householders took down the banners and folded them in tissue paper.

". . . so regal in her new dress."

"So clean. . . ."

". . . and such a healthy color!"

But Crome continued to look down the street for a long time after it was empty. Marguerite petals had fallen among the splashes of candle grease on the cobbled setts. He couldn't think how they came to be there. He picked some up in his hand and raised them to his face. A vivid recollection came to him of the smell of flowering privet in the suburbs of Soubridge when he was a boy, the late snapdragons and nasturtiums in the gardens. Suddenly he shrugged. He got directions to the narrow lane which would take him west of Alves to the Aqualate Pond, and having found it walked off up it rapidly. Fireworks burst from the arena, fizzing and flashing directly overhead; the walls of the houses danced and warped in the warm red light; his own shadow followed him along them, huge, misshapen, intermittent.

Crome shivered.

"Whatever is in the Aqualate Pond," Ingo Lympany the dramatist had once told him, "it's not water."

On the shore in front of a terrace of small shabby houses he had already found a kind of gibbet made of two great arched, bleached bones. From it swung a corpse whose sex he couldn't determine, upright in a tight wicker basket which creaked in the wind. The pond lay as still as Lympany had predicted, and it smelled of lead.

"Again, you see, everyone agrees it's a small pool, a very small one. But when you are standing by it, on the Henrietta Street side, you would swear that it stretched right off to the horizon. The winds there seem to have come such a distance. Because of this, the people in Henrietta Street believe they are living by an ocean, and make all the observances fishermen make. For instance, they say that a man can only die when the pool is ebbing. His bed must be oriented the same way as the floorboards, and at the moment of death doors and windows should be opened, mirrors covered with a clean white cloth, and all fires extinguished. And so on."

They believed too, at least the older ones did, that huge fish had once lived there.

"There are no tides, of course, and fish of any kind are rarely found there now. All the same, in Henrietta Street once a year they bring out a large stuffed pike, freshly varnished and with a bouquet of thistles in its mouth, and walk up and down the causeway with it, singing and shouting.

"And then—it's so hard to explain!—*echoes* go out over that stuff in the pool whenever you move, especially in the evening when the city is quiet: echoes and echoes of echoes, as though it were contained in some huge vacant metal building. But when you look up, there is only the sky."

"Well, Lympany," said Crome aloud to himself, "you were right."

He yawned. Whistling thinly and flapping his arms against his sides to keep warm, he paced to and fro underneath the gibbet. When he stood on the meager strip of pebbles at its edge, a chill seemed to seep out of the pool and into his bones. Behind him Henrietta Street stretched away, lugubrious and potholed. He promised himself, as he had done several times that night, that if he turned round and looked down it and still saw no one, he would go home. Afterward, he could never quite describe to himself what he had seen.

Fireworks flickered a moment in the dark, like the tremulous reflections made by a bath of water on the walls and ceilings of an empty room, and were gone. While they lasted Henrietta Street was all boarded-up windows and bluish shadows. He had the impression that, as he turned, it had just been vacated by a number of energetic figures—quiet, agile men who dodged into dark corners or flung themselves over the rotting fences and iron railings, or simply ran off very fast down the middle of the road *precisely so that he shouldn't see them.* At the same time he saw, or thought he saw, one real figure do all these things, as if it had been left behind by the rest, staring white-faced over its shoulder at him in total silence as it sprinted erratically from one feeble refuge to another, and then vanishing abruptly between some houses.

Overlaid, as it were, on both this action and the potential or completed action it suggested, was a woman in a brown cloak. At first she was tiny and distant, trudging up Henrietta Street toward him; then, without any transitional state at all, she appeared in the middle ground, posed like a piece of statuary between the puddles, white and naked, with one arm held up (behind her it was possible to glimpse for an instant three other women, but not to see what they were doing—except that they seemed to be plaiting flowers); finally with appalling suddenness, she filled his whole field of vision, as if on the Unter-Main-Kai a passerby had leaped in front of him without warning and screamed in his face. He gave a violent start and jumped backwards so quickly that he fell over. By the time he was able to get up, the sky was dark again, Henrietta Street empty, everything as it had been.

The woman, though, awaited him silently in the shadows beneath the gibbet, wrapped in her cloak like a sculpture wrapped in brown paper, and wearing over her head a complicated mask made of wafery metal to represent the head of one or another wasteland insect. Crome found that he had bitten his tongue. He approached her cautiously, holding out in front of him at arm's length the paper Verdigris had given him.

"Did you send me this?" he said.

"Yes."

"Do I know you?"

"No."

"What must I do to stop these dreams?"

She laughed. Echoes fled away over the Aqualate Pond.

"Kill the Mammy," she said.

Crome looked at her.

"You must be mad," he said. "Whoever you are."

"Wait," she recommended, "and we'll see who's mad."

She lowered the corpse in its wicker cage—the chains and pulleys of the gibbet gave a rusty creak—and pulled it toward her by its feet. Momentarily it escaped her and danced in a circle, coy and sad. She recaptured it with a murmur. "Hush, now. Hush." Crome backed away. "Look," he whispered, "I—" Before he could say anything else, she had slipped her hand deftly between the osiers and, like a woman gutting fish on a cold Wednesday morning at Lowth, opened the corpse from diaphragm to groin. "Man or woman?" she asked him, up to her elbows in it. "Which would you say?" A filthy smell filled the air and then dissipated. "I don't want—" said Crome. But she had already turned back to him and was offering him her hands, cupped, in a way that gave him no option but to see what she had found—or made—for him.

"Look!"

A dumb, doughy shape writhed and fought against itself on her palms, swelling quickly from the size of a dried pea to that of a newly born dog. It was, he saw, contained by vague and curious lights which came and went; then by a cream-colored fog which was perhaps only a blurring of its own spatial limits; and at last by a damp membrane, pink and gray, which it burst suddenly by butting and lunging. It was the lamb he had seen in his dreams, shivering and bleating and tottering in its struggle to stand, the eyes fixed on him forever in its complaisant, bone-white face. It seemed already to be sickening in the cold leaden breath of the Pond.

"Kill the Mammy," said the woman with the insect's

head, "and in a few days time you will be free. I will bring you a weapon soon."

"All right," said Crome.

He turned and ran.

He heard the lamb bleating after him the length of Henrietta Street, and behind that the sound of the sea, rolling and grinding the great stones in the tide.

For some days this image preoccupied him. The lamb made its way without fuss into his waking life. Wherever he looked he thought he saw it looking back at him: from an upper window in the Artists Quarter, or framed by the dusty iron railings which line the streets there, or from between the chestnut trees in an empty park.

Isolated in a way he had not been since he first arrived in Uroconium, wearing his green plush country waistcoat and yellow pointed shoes, he decided to tell no one what had happened by the Aqualate Pond. Then he thought he would tell Ansel Verdigris and Ingo Lympany. But Lympany had gone to Cladich to escape his creditors, and Verdigris, who after eating the tablecloth was no longer welcome at the Luitpold Café, had left the Quarter too. At the large old house in Delpine Square there was only his mother—a bit lonely in her bath chair, though still a striking woman with a great curved nose and a faint, heady smell of elder blossom—who said vaguely, "I'm sure I can remember what he said," but in the end could not.

"I wonder if you know, Ardwick Crome, how I worry about his *bowels*," she went on. "As his friend you must worry too, for they are very lazy, and he will not encourage them if we do not!"

It was, she said, a family failing.

She offered Crome chamomile tea, which he refused, and then got him to run an errand for her to a fashionable chemist's in Mynned. After that he could do nothing but go home and wait.

Kristodulos Fleece—half dead with opium and syphilis, and notoriously self-critical—had left behind him when he vacated the northlight studio a small picture. Traditionally, it remained there. Succeeding occupants had taken heart from its technical brio and uncustomary good humor (although Audsley King was reputed to have turned it to the wall during her brief period in Montrouge because she detected in it some unforgivable sentimentality or other), and no dealer in the Quarter would buy it for fear of bad luck. Crome now removed it to the corner above the cheap tin washstand so that he could see it from his bed.

Oil on canvas, about a foot square, it depicted in some detail a scene the artist had called "Children Beloved of the Gods Have the Power to Weep Roses." The children, mainly girls, were seen dancing under an elder tree, the leafless branches of which had been decorated with strips of rag. Behind them stretched away rough common land, with clumps of gorse and a few bare, graceful birch saplings, to where the upper windows and thatch of a low cottage could be made out. The lighthearted vigor of the dancers, who were winding themselves round the tallest girl in a spiral like a clock spring, was contrasted with the stillness of the late winter afternoon, its sharp clear airs and horizontal light. Crome had often watched this dance as a boy, though he had never been allowed to take part in it. He remembered the tranquil shadows on the grass, the chant, the rose and green colors of the sky. As soon as the dancers had wound the spiral tight, they would begin to tread on one another's toes, laughing and shrieking—or, changing to a different tune, jump up and down beneath the tree while one of them shouted, "A bundle of rags!"

It was perhaps as sentimental a picture as Audsley King had claimed. But Crome, who saw a lamb in every corner, had never seen one there; and when she came as she had promised, the woman with the insect's head found him gazing so quietly up at it from the trapezium of moonlight

falling across his bed that he looked like the effigy on a
tomb. She stood in the doorway, perhaps thinking he had
died and escaped her.

"I can't undo myself," he said.

The mask glittered faintly. Did he hear her breathing
beneath it? Before he could make up his mind, there was
a scuffling on the stairs behind her and she turned away to
say something he couldn't quite catch—though it might
have been: "Don't come in yourself."

"These straps are so old," he explained. "My father—"

"All right, give it to me, then," she said impatiently to
whoever was outside. "Now go away." And she shut the
door. Footsteps went down the stairs; it was so quiet in
Montrouge that you could hear them clearly going away
down flight after flight, scraping in the dust on a landing,
catching in the cracked linoleum. The street door opened
and closed. She waited, leaning against the door, until they
had gone off down the empty pavements toward Mynned
and the Ghibbeline Passage, then said, "I had better untie
you." But instead she walked over to the end of Crome's
bed, and sitting on it with her back to him stared thoughtfully
at the picture of the elder-tree dance.

"You were clever to find this," she told him. She stood
up again and, peering at it, ignored him when he said:

"It was in the other room when I came."

"I suppose someone helped you," she said. "Well, it
won't matter." Suddenly she demanded, "Do you like it
here among the rats? Why must you live here?"

He was puzzled.

"I don't know."

A shout went up in the distance, long and whispering
like a deeply drawn breath. Roman candles sailed up into
the night one after the other, exploding in the east below
the zenith so that the collapsing pantile roofs of Montrouge
stood out sharp and black. Light poured in, ran off the back

of the chair and along the belly of the enamel jug, and, discovering a book or a box here, a broken pencil there, threw them into merciless relief. Yellow or gold, ruby, greenish-white: with each new pulse the angles of the room grew more equivocal.

"Oh, it is the stadium!" cried the woman with the insect's head. "They have begun early tonight!"

She laughed and clapped her hands. Crome stared at her.

"Clowns will be capering in the great light!" she said.

Quickly she undid his straps.

"Look!"

Propped up against the whitewashed wall by the door, she had left a long brown paper parcel hastily tied with string. Fat or grease had escaped from it, and it looked as if it might contain a fish. While she fetched it for him, Crome sat on the edge of the bed with his elbows on his knees, rubbing his face. She carried it hieratically, across her outstretched arms, her image advancing and receding in the intermittent light.

"I want you to see clearly what we are going to lend you."

When the fireworks had stopped at last, an ancient white ceramic sheath came out of the paper. It was about two feet long, and it had been in the ground for a long time, yellowing to the color of ivory and collecting a craqueleure of fine lines like an old sink. Chemicals seeping through the soils of the Great Waste had left here and there on it faint blue stains. The weapon it contained had a matching hilt—although by now it was a much darker color from years of handling—and from the juncture of the two had leaked some greenish, jellylike substance which the woman with the insect's head was careful not to touch. She knelt on the bare floorboards at Crome's feet, her back and shoulders curved round the weapon, and slowly pulled hilt and sheath apart. At once a smell filled the room, thick and stale like wet

ashes in a dustbin. Pallid oval motes of light, some the size
of a birch leaf, others hardly visible, drifted up toward the
ceiling. They congregated in corners and did not disperse,
while the weapon, buzzing torpidly, drew a dull violet line
after it in the gloom as the woman with the insect's head
moved it slowly to and fro in front of her. She seemed to
be fascinated by it. Like all those things, it had been dug
up out of some pit. It had come to the city through the
Analeptic Kings, how long ago no one knew. Crome pulled
his legs up onto the bed out of its way.

"I don't want that," he said.

"Take it!"

"No."

"You don't understand. She is trying to change the name
of the city!"

"I don't want it. I don't care."

"Take it. Touch it. It's yours now."

"No!"

"Very well," she said quietly. "But don't imagine the
painting will help you again." She threw it on the bed near
him. "Look at it," she said. She laughed disgustedly. "'Children Beloved of the Gods...'!" she said. "Is that why he
waited for them outside the washhouses twice a week?"

The dance was much as it had been, but now with the
fading light the dancers had removed themselves to the
garden of the cottage, where they seemed frozen and awkward, as if they could only imitate the gaiety they had
previously felt. They were dancing in the shadow of the
bredogue which someone had thrust out of an open window
beneath the earth-colored eaves. In Soubridge, and in the
midlands generally, they make this pitiful thing—with its
bottle-glass eyes and crepe-paper harness—out of the
stripped and varnished skull of a horse, put up on a pole
covered with an ordinary sheet. This one, though, had the

skull of a well-grown lamb, which seemed to move as Crome looked.

"What have you done?" he whispered. "Where is the picture as it used to be?"

The lamb gaped its lower jaw slackly over the unsuspecting children to vomit on them its bad luck. Then, clothed with flesh again, it turned its white and pleading face on Crome, who groaned and threw the painting across the room and held out his hand.

"Give me the sword from under the ground, then," he said.

When the hilt of it touched his hand, he felt a faint sickly shock. The bones of his arm turned to jelly and the rank smell of ashpits enfolded him. It was the smell of a contient of wet cinders, buzzing with huge papery-winged flies under a poisonous brown sky; the smell of Cheminor, and Mammy Vooley, and the Aqualate Pond; it was the smell of the endless wastes which surround Uroconium and everything else that is left of the world. The woman with the insect's head looked at him with satisfaction. A knock came at the door.

"Go away!" she shouted. "You will ruin everything!"

"I'm to see that he's touched it," said a muffled voice. "I'm to make sure of that before I go back."

She shrugged impatiently and opened the door.

"Be quick, then," she said.

In came Ansel Verdigris, stinking of lemon geneva and wearing an extraordinary yellow satin shirt which made his face look like a corpse's. His coxcomb, freshly dyed that afternoon at some barber's in the Tinmarket, stuck up from his scalp in exotic scarlet spikes and feathers. Ignoring Crome and giving the woman with the insect's head only the briefest of placatory nods, he made a great show of looking for the weapon. He sniffed the air. He picked up the discarded sheath and sniffed that. (He licked his finger and went to touch the stuff that had leaked from it, but at the last moment he changed his mind.) He stared up at the vagrant motes of light in the corners of the room as if he could divine something from the way they wobbled and bobbed against the ceiling.

When he came to the bed he looked intently but with no sign of recognition into Crome's face.

"Oh, yes," he said. "He's touched it all right."

He laughed. He tapped the side of his nose, and winked. Then he ran round and round the room, crowing like a cock, his mouth gaping open and his tongue extended, until he fell over Kristodulos Fleece's painting, which lay against the baseboard where Crome had flung it. "Oh, he's touched it all right," he said, leaning exhaustedly against the door frame. He held the picture away from him at arm's length and looked at it with his head to one side. "Anyone could see that." His expression became pensive. "Anyone."

"The sword is in his hand," said the woman with the insect's head. "If you can tell us only what we see already, get out."

"It isn't you that wants to know," Verdigris answered flatly, as if he were thinking of something else. He propped the painting up against his thigh and passed the fingers of both hands several times rapidly through his hair. All at once he went and stood in the middle of the room on one leg, from which position he grinned at her insolently and began to sing in a thin musical treble, like a boy at a feast:

> "I choose you one, I choose you all,
> I pray I might go to the ball."

"Get out!" she shouted.

"The ball is mine," sang Verdigris,

"and none of yours,
Go to the woods and gather flowers.
Cats and kittens abide within
But we *court ladies* walk out and in!"

Some innuendo in the last line seemed to enrage her. She clenched her fists and brought them up to the sides of the mask, the feathery antennae of which quivered and trembled like a wasp's.

"Sting me!" taunted Verdigris. "Go on!"

She shuddered.

He tucked the painting under his arm and prepared to leave.

"Wait!" begged Crome, who had watched them with growing puzzlement and horror. "Verdigris, you must know that it is me! Why aren't you saying anything? What's happening?"

Verdigris, already in the doorway, turned round and gazed at Crome for a moment with an expression almost benign; then, curling his upper lip, he mimicked contemptuously, "'Verdigris, you've never *been* to Cheminor. *Neither* of us have.'" He spat on the floor and touched the phlegm he had produced with his toe, eyeing it with qualified disapproval. "Well, I have now, Crome. I have now." Crome saw that under their film of triumph his eyes were full of fear; his footsteps echoed down into the street and off into the ringing spaces of Montrouge and the Old City.

"Give the weapon to me," said the woman with the insect's head. As she put it back in its sheath, it gave out briefly the smells of rust, decaying horsehair, vegetable water. She seemed indecisive. "He won't come back," she said once. "I promise." But Crome would not look away from the wall. She went here and there in the room, blowing dust off a pile of books and reading a line or two in one of

them, opening the door into the northlight studio, then closing it again immediately, tapping her fingers on the edge
of the washstand. "I'm sorry about the painting," she said.
Crome could think of nothing to say to that. The floorboards
creaked; the bed moved. When he opened his eyes she was
lying next to him.

All the rest of the night her strange long body moved
over him in the unsteady illumination from the skylight.
The insect mask hung above him like a question, with its
huge faceted eyes and its jaws of filigree steel plate. He
heard her breath in it, distinctly, and once thought he saw
through it parts of her real face, pale lips, a cheekbone, an
ordinary human eye: but he would not speak to her.

The outer passages of the observatory at Alves are full
of an ancient grief. The light falls as if it has been strained
through muslin. The air is cold and moves unpredictably.
It is the grief of the old machines which, unfulfilled, whisper
suddenly to themselves and are silent again for a century.
No one knows what to do with them. No one knows how
to assuage them. A faint sour panic seems to cling to them:
they laugh as you go past, or extend a curious yellow film
of light like a wing.

"Ou lou lou," sounds from these passages almost daily—
more or less distant with each current of air—for Mammy
Vooley is often here. No one knows why. It is clear that
she herself is uncertain. If it is pride in her victory over the
Analeptic Kings, why does she sit alone in an alcove, staring
out of the windows? The Mammy who comes here to brood
is not the doll-like figure which processes the city on Fridays
and holidays. She will not wear her wig, or let them make
up her face. She is a constant trial to them. She sings quietly
and tunelessly to herself, and the plaster falls from the damp
ceilings into her lap. A dead mouse has now come to rest
there, and she will allow no one to remove it.

At the back of the observatory, the hill of Alves continues to rise a little. This knoll of ancient compacted rubbish, excavated into caves, mean dwellings, and cemeteries, is called Antedaraus because it drops away sheer into the Daraus Gorge. Behind it, on the western side of the gorge (which from above can be seen to divide Uroconium like a fissure in a wart), rise the ruinous towers of the Old City. Perhaps a dozen of them still stand, mysterious with spires and fluted moldings and glazed blue tiles, among the blackened hulks of those that fell during the City Wars. Every few minutes one or another of them sounds a bell, the feathery appeal of which fills the night from the streets below Alves to the shore of the Aqualate Pond, from Montrouge to the arena: in consequence the whole of Uroconium seems silent and tenantless—empty, littered, obscure, a city of expired fanaticisms.

Mammy Vooley hasn't time for those old towers, or for the mountains which rise beyond them to throw a shadow ten miles long across the bleak watersheds and shallow boggy valleys outside the city. It is the decayed terraces of the Antedaraus that preoccupy her. They are overgrown with mutant ivy and stifled whins; along them groups of mourners go, laden with anemones for the graves. Sour earth spills from the burst revetments between the beggars' houses, full of the rubbish of generations and strewn with dark red petals which give forth a sad odor in the rain. All day long the lines of women pass up and down the hill. They have with them the corpse of a baby in a box covered with flowers; behind them comes a boy dragging a coffin lid; they gossip endlessly. Mammy Vooley nods and smiles.

Everything her subjects do here is of interest to her: on the same evening that Crome found himself outside the observatory—fearfully clutching under his coat the weapon from the waste—she sat in the pervasive gloom somewhere in the corridors, listening with tilted head and lively eyes to a hoarse muted voice calling out from under the Ante-daraus. After a few minutes a man came out of a hole in the ground and with a great effort began pulling himself about in the sodden vegetation, dragging behind him a wicker basket of earth and excrement. He had, she saw, no legs. When he was forced to rest, he looked vacantly into the air; the rain fell into his face, but he didn't seem to notice it. He called out again. There was no answer. Eventually he emptied the basket and crawled back into the ground.

"Ah!" whispered Mammy Vooley, and sat forward expectantly.

She was already late; but she waved her attendants away when for the third time they brought her the wig and the wooden crown.

"Was it necessary to come here so publicly?" muttered Crome.

The woman with the insect's head was silent. When that morning he had asked her, "Where would you go if you could leave this city?" she had answered, "On a ship." And, when he stared at her, added, "In the night. I would find my father."

But now she only said:

"Hush. Hush, now. You will not be here long."

A crowd had been gathering all afternoon by the wide steps of the observatory. Ever since Mammy Vooley's arrival in the city it had been the custom for a group of young boys to dance on these steps on a certain day in November, in front of the gaunt wooden images of the Analeptic Kings. Everything was ready. Candles thickened the air with the smell of fat. The kings had been brought out, and now loomed inert in the gathering darkness, their immense defaced heads lumpish and threatening. The choir could be heard from inside the observatory, practicing and coughing, practicing and coughing, under that dull cracked dome which absorbs every echo like felt. The little boys—they were seven or eight years old—huddled together on the seeping stones, pale and grave in their outlandish costumes. They were coughing too in the dampness that creeps down every winter from the Antedaraus.

"The weapon is making me ill," said Crome. "What must I do? Where is she?"

"Hush."

At last the dancers were allowed to take their places about halfway up the steps, where they stood in a line looking nervously at one another until the music signaled them to begin. The choir was marshaled and sang its famous "Renunciative" cantos, above which rose the whine of the cor anglais and the thudding of a large flat drum. The little boys revolved slowly in simple, strict figures, with expressions inturned and languid. For every two paces forward, it had been decreed, they must take two back.

Soon Mammy Vooley was pushed into view at the top of the steps, in a chair with four iron wheels. Her head lolled against its curved back. Attendants surrounded her immediately, young men and women in stiff embroidered robes who, after a perfunctory bow, set about ordering her wisp of hair or arranging her feet on a padded stool. They held a huge book up in front of her single milky eye, and then placed in her lap the crown or wreath of woven yew twigs which she would later throw to the dancing boys. Throughout the dance she stared uninterestedly up into the sky, but as soon as it was finished and they had helped her to sit up she proclaimed in a distant yet eager voice:

"Even these were humbled."

She made them open the book in front of her again, at a different page. She had brought it with her from the north.

"Even these kings were made to bend the knee," she read.

The crowd cheered.

She was unable after all to throw the wreath, although her hands picked disconnectedly at it for some seconds. In the end it was enough for her to let it slip out of her lap and fall among the boys, who scrambled with solemn faces down the observatory steps after it while her attendants showered them with crystallized geranium petals and other colored sweets, and in the crowd their parents urged them, "Quick now!"

The rain came on in earnest, putting out some of the candles; the wreath rolled about on the bottom step like a coin set spinning on a table in the Luitpold Café, then toppled over and was still. The quickest boy had claimed it, Mammy Vooley's head had fallen to one side again, and they were preparing to close the great doors behind her when shouting and commotion broke out in the observatory itself and a preposterous figure in a yellow satin shirt burst onto the steps near her chair. It was Ansel Verdigris. He had spewed blackcurrant gin down his chest, and his coxcomb, now disheveled and lax, was plastered across his sweating forehead like a smear of blood. He still clutched under one arm the painting he had taken from Crome's room. This he began to wave about in the air above his head with both hands so strenuously that the frame broke and the canvas flapped loose from it.

"Wait!" he shouted.

The woman with the insect's head gave a great sideways jump of surprise, like a horse. She stared at Verdigris for a second as if she didn't know what to do, then pushed Crome in the back with the flat of her hand.

"Now!" she hissed urgently. "Go and kill her now or it will be too late!"

"What?" said Crome.

As he fumbled at the hilt of the weapon, poison seemed to flow up his arm and into his neck. Whitish motes leaked out of the front of his coat and, stinking of the ashpit, wobbled heavily past his face up into the damp air. The people nearest him moved away sharply, their expressions puzzled and nervous.

"Plotters are abroad," Ansel Verdigris was shouting, "in this very crowd!"

He looked for some confirmation from the inert figure of Mammy Vooley, but she ignored him and only gazed exhaustedly into space while the rain turned the breadcrumbs in her lap to paste. He squealed with terror and threw the painting on the floor.

"People stared at this picture," he said. He kicked it. "They knelt in front of it. They have dug up an old weapon and wait now to kill the Mammy!"

He sobbed. He caught sight of Crome.

"Him!" he shouted. "There! There!"

"What has he done?" whispered Crome.

He dragged the sword out from under his coat and threw away its sheath. The crowd fell back immediately, some of them gasping and retching at its smell. Crome ran up the steps holding it out awkwardly in front of him, and hit Ansel Verdigris on the head with it. Buzzing dully, it cut down through the front of Verdigris's skull, then, deflected by the bridge of his nose, skidded off the bony orbit of the eye and hacked into his shoulders. His knees buckled and his arm on that side fell of. He went to pick it up and then changed his mind, glaring angrily at Crome instead and working the glistening white bones of his jaw. "Bugger," he said. "Ur." He marched unsteadily about at the top of the steps, laughing and pointing at his own head.

"I wanted this," he said thickly to the crowd. "It's just what I wanted!" Eventually he stumbled over the painting, fell down the steps with his remaining arm swinging out loosely, and was still.

Crome turned round and tried to hit Mammy Vooley with the weapon, but he found that it had gone out like a wet firework. Only the ceramic hilt was left—blackened, stinking of fish, giving out a few gray motes which moved around feebly and soon died. When he saw this he was so relieved that he sat down. An enormous tiredness seemed to have settled in the back of his neck. Realizing that they were safe, Mammy Vooley's attendants rushed out of the observatory and dragged him to his feet again. One of the first to reach him was the woman with the insect's head.

"I suppose I'll be sent to the arena now," he said.

"I'm sorry."

He shrugged.

"The thing seems to be stuck to my hand," he told her. "Do you know anything about it? How to get it off?"

But it was his hand, he found, that was at fault. It had swollen into a thick clubbed mass the color of over-cooked mutton, in which the hilt of the weapon was now embedded. He could just see part of it protruding. If he shook his arm, waves of numbness came up it; it did no good anyway; he couldn't let go.

"I hated my rooms," he said. "But I wish I was back in them now."

"I was betrayed too, you know," she said.

Later, while two women supported her head, Mammy Vooley peered into Crome's face as if trying to remember where she had seen him before. She was trembling, he noticed, with fear or rage. Her eye was filmed and watery, and a smell of stale food came up out of her lap. He expected her to say something to him, but she only looked and after a short time signed to the women to push her away. "I forgive all my subjects," she announced to the crowd. "Even this one." As an afterthought she added, "Good news! Henceforth this city will be called Vira Co, 'the City in the Waste.'" Then she had the choir brought forward. As he was led away Crome heard it strike up "Ou lou, lou," that ancient song:

Ou lou   lou lou
Ou lou lou
Ou lou   lou lou
Ou lou lou
Ou lou   lou lou
Lou lou   lou lou
Ou lou   lou lou

Lou
Lou
Lou

Soon the crowd was singing too.

The Lords of Misrule

"WE MAY SOON BE overrun," the Yule Greave said, looking away over the empty moorland and rough grazing seamed with tree-filled cloughs. "Aid from the city is our only hope now."

He was a tall man, fortyish, with weak blue eyes and a straggle of thin blond hair, who breathed laboriously through his mouth. Under the old queen, who had given him the house and the pasture that went with it, he had been known as a fighter. Every so often he would look around him as if surprised to find himself where he was, and his lower lip trembled briefly when he talked about the city.

To give him time to catch his breath, I stopped and looked back down at the house. It was built on a curious pattern, like an ideogram from an old language, ramified, peculiar. Much of it now lay abandoned and overgrown in a tangle of elder and hawthorn and ivy. Flung out from it were four great stone avenues, each a mile long. I wondered who had built them, and when.

"I've been forced to knock down some of the walls and grub up the pavement," he said. "But you can see what it was once like."

There were deep muddy furrows in the gateways where the stone-carts went in and out. The wind came in gusts from the south and west, bringing a rainy smell and the distant bleat of sheep. The dwarf oaks on the slopes above us shifted their branches uneasily and sent down a few more of last winter's brownish withered leaves. One of the little gray hawks of the moorland launched itself from some rocks above us, planing downwind with its wingtips ragged against the racing white clouds; it hovered for a moment, then veered off and dropped like a stone onto something in the bracken below.

"Look!" I said.

The Yule Greave stood wiping his face and nodding vaguely.

"To tell you the truth," he said, "we never thought they would come this far. We expected you people to stop them long before this."

I breathed in the smell of the bracken. "This is such a beautiful valley," I said.

"You'll be able to see the whole of it soon," the Yule Greave said. He started up the slope where it steepened for its final climb to the rim of the escarpment, following a soft, peaty sheep-trod through the bracken. He placed one foot carefully and heavily in front of the others, grunting at the steeper places and still breathing heavily. "I'm sorry to bring you all this way," he said. "I don't expect you're used to this sort of thing."

"I'm not tired," I said.

He laughed, his blue eyes watering unoffendedly. "You really have to see it from up here," he said, "to appreciate the position. You'll be able to judge for yourself how far they've come."

"Of course."

We climbed the last few yards to the little outcrop in silence. At the top, when I turned, the spring sun had come out briefly, and I could feel it on my face. It was three or four minutes before the Yule Greave recovered himself suf-

ficiently to speak. Sweat poured down his forehead and into
his eyes, which were sore in the dusty wind. He put one
hand against the rock to steady himself. "They quarried this
to build the house," he said. "A long time ago."

The rock was pale, coarse-textured, full of little quartz
pebbles. Higher up in the quarried bays hung mats of ivy.

"Now you can see what I mean," he said.

Below us the house lay like a metaphor in the wide flat
valley. It was a light fawn color. Its four vast avenues of
stone thrust out from it across the old alluvial bench, black,
black. What it meant I had no idea. It was one of those
places where the past speaks to us in a language so completely of its own that we have no hope of understanding.
Puddles of water in the worn paving reflected the sky; I
could see gaps in the tall walls like bites, where the Yule
Greave had taken stone for his fortifications, a line of hasty
revetments and trenches stretching across the valley lower
down, where it sloped away to the south.

"Incredible," I said.

He pointed south, past the fortifications.

"There used to be a dozen houses like this," he said
bitterly. "And places even older than this. But all overrun
now, and the decent people who lived there gone. All the
way down to the sea you could find houses like this, full
of decent people."

Anger glittered moistly in his eyes.

"What do we make, we who come after? Nothing! We
pull it all down instead."

"I'm not sure I agree," I said, tempted to ask him why,
if he didn't want to destroy the old walls, he didn't reopen
the quarry and use fresh stone; but his face was now full
of a kind of savage self-hatred and self-pity, and he said:

"What's the point of discussing it? Everything's gone to
waste. It was all up a thousand years ago for the people
who built this."

Abruptly he shrugged and apologized.

"You've heard it all before, I expect. Anyway, you can see how close they've come. They'll be across the river and over the fortifications in a month, perhaps less if we don't get help. See: there, and there? You can see the sun glinting on their camps."

"Will you show me the house before I go?" I asked.

He looked at me in surprise. He was pleased to be asked, I thought, but he said, "Oh, the inside's a ruin now. We do our best, but it's all dust and mice."

He seemed reluctant to go down the hill now that he had got up it. He watched the little gray hawk hovering and stooping, hovering and stooping, as it worked its way up and down the slopes of sun-warmed bracken. He took a last look at the great stone symbol which filled the valley and which he had lived in for twenty years without understanding, then began to descend slowly. New shoots, he observed, were beginning to appear green and delicately curled between the ruined bracken stems. The turf, flattened and bleached by the previous months' snow, was springing up again. "That air!" he exclaimed, breathing ecstatically a gust of wind which brought the scent of May blossom up from the valley. Then he stopped suddenly and said, "How is it in the city these days?"

I shrugged.

"We have similar problems to yours," I heard myself tell him, "but not so extreme. Otherwise it is very beautiful. New buildings are springing up everywhere. The horse chestnuts are in blossom along the Margarethestrasse and in the Plaza of Unrealized Time."

I did not mention the torn political cartoons flapping from the rusty iron railings, or the Animal Mask Societies with their public rituals and increasingly unreasonable demands. But he was remembering a different city anyway.

"I suppose the place is still full of clerks and shopkeepers?" he said. "And tarts who overcharge you in the Rue Ouled Nail?"

He laughed.

"We'll always look to Uroconium," he said sentimentally, and quoted, "'Queen of the Empire, jewel on the beach of the Western Sea.'"

The high walls that surrounded the house had already warmed to the weak sunshine, trapping a fraction of its heat to give up to the elder and ivy in the overgrown gardens. Two or three hawthorns filled the air with the scent of the may, which in that confined space seemed drugged and dangerous. Insects murmured in the little orchard and among the fruit bushes which had run to bramble in the shelter of the walls. Above the garden rose the heavy honey-colored stone of the main building, covered in creeper and bright yellow lichens. The wind blustered round its complicated roofs.

Inside the house he had someone bring out a bottle of lemon geneva, and invited me to have some.

"Foul stuff, but the best we can get out here."

We drank silently for a while. The Yule Greave grew pinker in the face, more irritable. He seemed to sink into himself, into his own sense of abandonment and futility. "Dust and mice," he said, staring round in disgust at the high gloomy walls and the silent, massive, oppressive old furniture, "dust and rats. This is the only room we ever light a fire in." Later he began to talk about the old queen's reign. It was the common story of infighting at court and violence in the city. Many of the actions in which he had taken part struck me as being little more than outrages, committed by people hardly able to help themselves. He kept his souvenirs of these "little wars" in one of the upperrooms, he said. There was some peculiar stuff among it all, stuff that made you think. We could go and look at it later if I was interested.

"I'd like that if there's time," I said.

"Oh, there'll be time," he said. "It's mostly clothes, weapons, stuff we picked up in their houses. You wouldn't credit the hanks of hair, the filthy pictures they were always looking at."

He asked if I had done any fighting in the city, and I said that I hadn't. There was a silence, then he went on musingly: "The women were the worst. They would hide in doorways, and reach out for your face or your neck as you walked past. Hide themselves in doorways. They'd have bits of glass embedded in a cake of soap, do you see, and slash out at your neck or your eyes." He looked at me as if he were wondering how much more he could tell me. "Can you believe that?" He shook his head. "I hated going up the stairs in those places. The lamps would all be out. You never knew what would be in a cupboard. A woman or a child, screaming at you. Or else they'd show you something foul, something obscene, and laugh. The old queen would never bear them near her, not at any price."

"So I have heard," I said. "It is less of a problem now."

He chuckled.

"Old men like me cleared it up for you," he said. "We can be proud of that."

A little later his wife came in. By this time he had drunk most of the bottle. He stared at her with a kind of muddled resentment.

She was a tall woman, though not perhaps as tall as him, very thin and ethereal, dressed in a fashion long out of date in the city. She seemed not quite real to me, like a picture in a darkened room. I guessed she had been one of the old queen's women-in-waiting, given to him like the house and the valley in return for his loyalty in the backstreets and tavern brawls. Her hair, an astonishing orange color, was worn long and crimped, to emphasize the height of her cheekbones, the whiteness of her skin, and the odd, concave curve of her features.

Over one arm she was carrying a piece of heavily embroidered cloth which I recognized as being part of the "mast horse" ceremony: it would be used to hide the operator of the animal's snapping jaw. I had never seen such an elaborate cloth in use. When I mentioned this she smiled and said:

"You'll have to ask Ringmer if you want to know more about it. He was born near here, and his father worked the horse at All Hallows."

"Ringmer's father was a half-wit," said the Yule Greave, yawning and pouring himself more lemon gin.

She ignored him. "Are you young men at all interested in such things in the city now?" she asked me. Her eyes were green. She had unfolded the cloth to show me a complex pattern of leaflike shapes.

"Yes," I said. "Some are."

"Because I've filled a whole gallery with them. Ringmer—"

"Has he shifted the rubble in the south avenue?" the Yule Greave broke in suddenly.

"I don't know."

"It was important to get that rubble moved today," the Yule Greave said. "I want it as infill further down the valley. I told him this morning."

"He didn't tell me that's what he was supposed to be doing," she said.

The Yule Greave muttered something I couldn't quite catch and emptied his glass quickly. He got up and stared out at the ruined raspberry canes and lichen-covered apple boughs in the garden, his hands trembling. This left me marooned with his wife at the other end of the long room, with only the embroidered cloth in common. A few transparent blue and orange flames stirred round the unseasoned logs in the hearth.

"Ringmer will show you the rest of the horse, if you'd like to see it," she said. "I'm so glad you're interested."

She folded the fabric up again, her long thin hands white in the shadows. "Sometimes I feel like wearing it myself," she laughed, holding it up against her shoulders. "It's so glorious!" I had a brief vision of her as she must have been in the days of the old queen's court—waxy and still in a stiff, gray, heavily embossed garment down to her feet, like a flower in a steel vase. Then the Yule Greave came and stood between us to tip into his glass whatever dregs remained in the brown stone bottle. He was breathing heavily again, as if ascending some private hill.

"Don't you want to come up and see the things I told you about?" he said.

"I shouldn't stay more than a few minutes," I answered. "My men will be waiting for me—"

"But you've only just arrived!"

"I have to be in Uroconium by tomorrow morning."

"He wants to see the horse, whatever else," the Yule Greave's wife insisted.

"Oh, does he? You'd better go and show him, then," he said, looking at me as if I had let him down and then turning abruptly away. He poked so hard at the fire that one of the logs fell out of it. Smoke came into the room in a thick cloud. "This stinking chimney!" he shouted.

We left the room, the Yule Greave looking after us red-faced and watery-eyed. The "gallery," which was some distance away, turned out to be a mezzanine floor somewhere in the west wing. The sun was just coming round to it, pouring obliquely in through the tall lanceolate windows. The Yule Greave's wife stood in an intermittent pool of warm yellow light with her hands clasped anxiously.

"Ringmer?" she called. "Ringmer?"

We stood and listened to the wind blustering about outside.

After a moment, a boy of twenty or so came out of the shadows of the mezzanine. He looked surprised to see her.

He had the thick legs and shoulders of the moorland people, and the characteristic soft brown hair chopped off to a line above his raw-looking ears. He was carrying a horse's head on a pole.

"I see you have the rest of the Mari," she said with a smile. "Do you think you could show our guest? I've brought the coat back with me."

It was an astonishing specimen. Usually you find the skull boiled and crudely varnished, or buried for a year to get rid of the flesh, a makeshift wire hinge for the jaw, and the bottoms of cheap green bottles for eyes. This one had been made long ago, and with more care: it was lacquered black, its jaw was hinged with massive silver rivets, and somehow the inside of a pomegranate had been preserved and inserted, half in each orbit, so that the seeds made bulging, faceted eyes. It must have been appallingly heavy for the operator. The pole on which it rested was brown bone, three and a half feet long and polished with use.

"It is very striking," I said.

The boy now took the embroidered cloth and shook it out. Hooks fitted along its top edge allowed it to be gathered beneath the horse's head so that it fell in stiff folds and obscured the pole. With a quick, agile movement he slipped under it and crouched down. The Mari came to life, hump-backed, curvetting, and snapping its jaw. It predated not only the Yule Greave but his house. Time opened like a hole underneath us, and the Yule Greave's wife stepped back suddenly.

"'Open the door for us,'" chanted the boy:

> "It is cold outside for the gray mare
> Its heels are almost frozen."

"I would admit you at my peril," I said. The Yule Greave's wife laughed.

I went to examine some manuscripts which belonged to the house. They were kept at the other end of the mezzanine. When I looked back the Yule Greave's wife was standing next to the mast horse. Its eyes glittered, its lower jar hung down. Her hand was resting on its back, just as it might rest on the neck of a real animal, and she was saying something to it in a low voice. I never found out what, because at that moment the Yule Greave came puffing and panting into the gallery, limping as if he had banged his leg and shouting, "All right, come on, you've seen enough of this."

The Mari reared up for a second, bared its white teeth, then retreated into the shadows, and the boy Ringmer with it.

At the door of the staircase which led to the Yule Greave's private room I took my leave of his wife, in case, as she said, we did not meet again. "I'm sorry we have badgered you so," she said. "We see so few people."

I laughed.

"Hurry up," urged the Yule Greave. "It's quite a climb."

The staircase was so narrow that he rubbed his shoulders on the walls as he led the way up, brushing off great flakes of damp yellow plaster. His fat pear-shaped buttocks shut out the light. The little square room was right at the top of the house. From its narrow windows you could see one of the stone avenues stretching away, a silver of brownish hillside, and a bend in the shallow stony river. The wind boomed around us, bringing quite clearly the bleat of moorland sheep.

The Yule Greave tried to open a trap door in the ceiling so that we could go out onto the roof, which was flat here. The bolts were rusted shut, but he would give up only after a lot of heaving and grunting.

"I can't understand it," he said. "I'm sorry."

He hammered at one of the bolts until he cut the heel of his hand, then his eyes watered and he began to cry. He turned away from me and pretended to look out across the hillside, where the sheep were scattered like gray rocks.

"You'd never believe we were abandoning these old places," he said. "Simply abandoning them one by one. The future will judge us very harshly." He sniffed and blinked. He looked at his cut hand, then wiped his eyes with it, leaving a smear of blood. "Now look what I've done. I'm sorry."

I couldn't think of anything to say.

The tower smelled of the old books he had abandoned to the mold in haphazard piles. I picked up *Oei'l Voirrey* and *The Death and Revival of the Earl of Rone*. I asked him if he would show me his souvenirs, but he seemed to have lost interest. He kept them in a wooden chest: a few dolls made out of women's hair and bits of mirror; some cooking implements; a knife of curious design. The damp had got at everything and made it worthless. "It's just the sort of thing we all picked up," he said. "I think there's a mask in there somewhere."

"'The men of the community set out in the afternoon,'" I quoted, "'and, after much parading and searching, discover the Earl of Rone hidden ineffectually in the low scrub...'"

"You can keep the *Oei'l Voirrey* if you like," he said.

We stared down at the ancient avenue stretching away from the house, its puddled surface reflecting the white sky. His wife appeared walking slowly along it with the boy Ringmer. They were smiling and talking. The Yule Greave watched them sadly, biting his nails, until I said that I would have to go.

"You must at least have something to eat with us," he said.

"I have to be in the city before morning," I said. "I'm sorry."

We went down the stairs and he came out to say goodbye. There was no sign of his wife. I got on my horse in one of the muddy gateways. As I set off down the long avenue I thought I heard him say, "Tell them in the city that we still keep faith."

The avenue seemed barren and endless. The sun had gone in and it was raining again by the time I led my men through a break in one of the walls; and with the cold wind of spring blowing into our backs, we turned north and picked our way up to the rim of the escarpment.

Up by the Yule Greave's abandoned quarries I stopped to have one more look at the house. It seemed silent and untenanted. Then I saw a stone-cart move slowly down the valley toward the fortifications. Smoke came out of one of the chimneys. Above me the little gray hawk dipped and swerved on the wind. My men, sensing my preoccupation, huddled in a bay of the quarry, wrapped in their sodden cloaks and talking quietly. I could smell moorland, wet wool, the breath of the horses. Soon most of the valley was obscured by mist and driving rain, but I could see the fortifications lying across it in raw straight lines, and beyond them, toward the sea where a fugitive and watery sun was still shining, the light was reflected off the waiting encampments.

If I had the eyes of that hawk, I thought, I know what I would see down there, moving toward us from the sea.

One of my men pointed to the fortifications and said, "Those walls won't last long, however well they're defended."

I found myself staring at him for a long time before answering.

Then I said, "They have already been breached. That house down there is raddled."

Even as we watched, the Yule Greave and his wife and their three children came out of the house with the boy Ringmer, and began to dance in a circle in the overgrown

garden. I could hear the thin voices of the children carrying
the tune, blown up the hill with the mist and the rain:

> "What time will the king come home?
> One o'clock in the afternoon.
> What will he have in his hand?
> A bunch of ivy."

Behind me someone said, "You've dropped your book,
sir."

"Let it lie."

In Viriconium

ASHLYME THE PORTRAIT painter, of whom it had once been said that he "first put his sitter's soul in the killing bottle, then pinned it out on the canvas for everyone to look at like a broken moth," kept a diary. One night he wrote in it:

"The plague zone has undergone one of its periodic internal upheavals and extended its boundaries another mile. I would care as little as anyone else up here in the High City if it were not for Audsley King. Her rooms above the Rue Serpolet now fall within its influence. She is already ill. I am not sure what to do."

He was a strange little man to have got the sort of reputation he had. At first sight his clients, who often described themselves later as victims, thought little of him. His wedge-shaped head was topped by a coxcomb of red hair which gave him a queer shocked expression. His face accentuated this, being pale and bland of feature, except the eyes which were very large and wide. He wore the ordinary clothes of the time, and one steel ring he had been told was valuable. He had few close friends in the city. He came from a family of rural landlords somewhere in the south; no one knew them. (This accident of birth had entitled him to wear a sword, but he never bothered. He had one somewhere, in a cupboard. He did carry a short knife, using it mainly to sharpen pencils. It had a queer flaw in the blade which rendered it useless for anything else.)

Despite the cruelty of his portraits, he was not misanthropic, and had no great passion for truth. These, his acquaintances remarked, must reside—if anywhere—in his pallet or brushes.

"She must be got out of there," he continued, writing a little more quickly. "I have thought of nothing else since this evening's meeting with Paulinus Rack. Rack, with his fat lips and intimate asides! In his oily hands he had some proof sketches for her designs for *The Dreaming Boys*— *Die Traumunden Knaben*. I stared at them and knew that she must be preserved. They are inexplicable, these figures in their trancelike yet painful attitudes. They suggest a form and line quite foreign to us warmer, more human beings. Could she have understood something about the nature of the crisis that we have not?"

He bit his pen.

"But how to persuade her to leave? And how to persuade anyone to help me?"

This was rhetoric. He had already persuaded Emmet Buffeau the astronomer to help him. But what is a diary for, if not effect? The world has already seen too much history recorded: that was the unconsciously held belief of his age.

When the ink was dry he locked the book, then picked up the light easel he used for preliminary studies and went down the stairs. "Come sometimes at night," she had said when he accepted the commission—and laughed. "A lamp can be as unflattering as daylight." (Touching his sleeve with one mannish hand.) At the bottom of the stairs he stood still for a second or two, then let himself out into the empty street and echoing night. From here he had a view of the Low City, some odd quality of the moonlight giving back any foreground planes equal value, so that it had no perspective but was just a clutter of blue and gamboge roofs filling the space between his eyes and the hills outside the city. He made his way down to it.

In those days a thousand steps led down from the heights of Mynned, hidden behind the facade of the Margarethe-strasse and its triumphal arches, winding among the fish markets and pie shops where the Artists Quarter rubs up against the High City like someone's old unwanted animal. There were people who did not want to be seen coming and going between High City and Low. They could be heard ascending and descending this stairway all night, among them those curious twin princes of the city, the Beezley brothers. (How are we to explain them? They weren't human, that's a fact. Had Ashlyme known his fate was mixed up with theirs, would he have been more careful in the plague zone?) At the bottom they would let themselves through a small iron gate. It was constructed so as to permit only one person through at a time, and its name commem-orated in the Low City some atrocity long since forgotten in the High. Ashlyme had his own reasons for keeping off the Margarethestrasse. Perhaps his nightly visits to the Rue Serpolet embarrassed him.

He was inclined to hurry through the Artists Quarter. He did not know it well, and he had never quite liked what he thought of as its "secessionist" atmosphere.

Blue light leaked from the chromium doors of the bras-series as he passed. In the Bistro Californium, beneath Kris-todulos's notorious frescoes, some desperate celebration was in progress. Out came the high-pitched voice of a poet, auctioning the dull things he had found in the back of his brain. There was a peculiar laugh, a scatter of applause, silence. Further on, in the Plaza of Unrealized Time, beggars were lounging outside the rooms of the women, curious bandages accentuating rather than covering their deformities as they relaxed after the day. One or two of them winked or smiled at him. Ashlyme clutched his easel and quickened his pace until they had fallen behind. In this way, quite soon, he entered the infected zone.

The plague is difficult to describe. It had begun some months before. It was not a plague in the ordinary sense of the word. It was a kind of thin-ness, a transparency. Within it people aged quickly, or succumbed to debilitating ill-nesses—influenza, phthisia, galloping consumption. The very buildings fell apart and began to look unkempt, ill-kept. Businesses failed. All projects dragged out indefinitely but came in the end to nothing.

If you went up into the foothills, claimed Emmet Buf-feau, and looked down into the city through a telescope, you could see the affected zone spreading like a thin fog. "The instrument reveals something quite new!" The Low City streets, the people you could see in them (and he had an instrument which enabled them to be seen quite clearly) were a little faded or blurred, as if the light were bad or the lenses grimy. But if you turned the identical telescope on the pastel towers and great plazas of the High City, they stood out as bright and sharp as a bank of flowers in the sun. "It is not the light at fault, after all, or the instrument!" Whether you believed him or not, few areas south of the Boulevard Aussman remained safe; and to the southeast the periphery of the infection now threatened the High City itself along the line of the Margarethestrasse, bulging a little to accommodate the warren of defeated avenues, small ren-tier apartments, and vegetable markets which lay beneath the hill at Alves. Buffeau's observations might or might not be reliable. In any case they only told part of the story. The rest lay in the Low City, and to appreciate it you had to go there.

Ashlyme, who was there and didn't appreciate it, put down his easel and massaged his elbow. With the onset of the plague, all the streets in this corner of the city had begun to seem the same, lined with identical dusty chestnut trees and broken metal railings. He had walked down the Rue Serpolet ten minutes ago, he discovered, without recognizing it. The houses on either side of Audsley King's were empty. Piles of plaster and lath and hardened mortar lay everywhere, evidence of grandiose and complicated repairs which, like the schemes of the rentiers who had instituted them, would never be completed. Speculation of this kind was feverish in the plague zone: a story was told in the High City in which a whole street changed hands three times in one week, its occupants remaining lethargic and uninterested.

Audsley King had a confusing suite of rooms on an upper floor. The stairs smelled faintly of geraniums and dried orange peel. Ashlyme stood uncertainly on the landing with a cat sniffing round his feet. "Hello?" he called. He never knew what to expect of her. Once, she had sprung out on him from a closet, laughing helplessly. He could hear low voices coming from one of the rooms, but he wasn't sure which. He set his easel down loudly on the bare boards. The cat ran off. "It's Ashlyme," he said. He went from room to room, looking for her. They were full of paintings propped up against the dull cream walls. He found himself staring down into a square garden like a cistern, full of darkness and trailing plants. "I'm here!" he called—but was he? She made him feel like a ghost, swimming idly around, waiting to be noticed. He opened what he thought was a cupboard, but it turned out to be a short hall with a green velvet curtain at the end of it, which gave on to her studio.

She was sitting there on the floor with Fat Mam Etteilla, the fortune-teller and cardsharp. One lamp gave out a yellow light which was reflected from the upturned cards—threw the women themselves into prominence—but failed to light the rest of the room, which was quite large. Consequently, they seemed to be posed in their strained and graceless attitudes against a yellow emptiness in which hung only the faintest suggestions of objects—a pot of anemones, the corner of an easel, or a window frame. This lent a bewildering ambiguity to the scene he was later to paint from memory as "Visiting the Women in Their Upper Room." In the picture we see the Fat Mam sitting with her skirts pulled up to her thighs and her legs spread out, facing the cards (these are without symbols and, though arranged for divination, predict nothing). Crouched between her thighs and also facing the cards is a much thinner woman with hair cropped like an adolescent boy's and a body all elbows and knees. Ashlyme's treatment of these figures is extraordinary. Their arms are locked together, and they seem to be rocking to and fro—in grief, perhaps, or in the excesses of some strange and joyless sexual spasm. A few brutal lines contain them; all else is void. There is some humanity in the way he has colored the skirts of the Fat Mam. But Audsley King is looking defiantly out of the canvas, her eyes sly.

They remained in this position for thirty seconds or so after he had pulled back the curtain. The studio was quiet but for the hoarse breathing of the fortune-teller. Audsley King smiled sleepily at Ashlyme; then, when he said nothing, reached out deliberately and disarranged the cards. Suddenly she began coughing. She put her hand hurriedly over her mouth and turned her head away, writhing her thin shoulders in the attempt to expel something. "Oh, go away, you old fool," she said indistinctly to the fortune-teller. "You can see it hasn't worked." When Ashlyme took her hand it was full of blood. He helped her to a chair and made her comfortable while the Fat Mam put away the cards, brought water, lit the other lamps.

"How tired I am," said Audsley King, smiling up at him, "of hearing my lung creak all day like a new boot." She wiped her mouth with the back of her hand. "It makes me so impatient."

The hemorrhage had left her disoriented but demanding, like a child waking up in the middle of a long journey. She forgot Ashlyme's name, or pretended to. But she would not let him leave, she would not hear of it. He would set up his easel like a proper painter and work on the portrait. Meanwhile she would entertain him with anecdotes, and the Fat Mam would read his fortune in the cards. They would make him tea or chocolate, whichever he preferred.

Ashlyme, though, had never seen her so pale. Should she not go to bed? She would have her portrait painted. In the face of such determination, what else could he do but admire her harsh, mannish profile and white cheeks, and comply? After he had been drawing for about an hour, he put down the black chalk and said carefully:

"If you would just come to the High City. Rack is a charlatan, but he would have you well cared for—if only to safeguard his investment."

"Ashlyme, you promised me."

"It will soon be too late. The quarantine police."

"It's already too late." She moved her shoulders fretfully. "You stupid man. The plague is here"—indicating herself and then the room at large, with its morose draped furniture and empty picture frames—"and in here. It hangs in the street down there like a fog. They will make no exceptions." For a moment a terrible hunger lit up her eyes. But it turned slowly into indifference. "Besides," she said, "I would not go if they did. Why should I go? The High City is an elaborate catafalque. Art is dead up there, and Paulinus Rack is burying it. I no longer wish to go there." Her voice rose. "I no longer wish them to buy my work. I belong here."

Ashlyme would have argued further. She said she would cough herself to death if he did. He went miserably back to his task.

A curious listlessness now came over the studio—the dull, companionable silence of the plague zone, which stretched time out like a thread of mucus. Mam Etteilla shuffled the cards. (What was she doing here, this fat, patient woman, away from her grubby satin booth in the Plaza of Unrealized Time? What arrangement had been made between them?) She set the cards out, read them, gathered them up without a word. She did this sitting on the floor, while Audsley King looked on expressionlessly, for the present indifferent to her own condition, as if she were dreaming it. The feverish energy of the hemorrhage seemed to have left her; she had sunk into her chair, eyes half-closed. Only once did the symbols on the cards attract her attention. She leaned forward and said:

"As a young girl I lived on a farm. It was somewhere in the damp, endless plowland near Soubridge. Every week my father killed and plucked three chickens. They hung on the back of a door until they were eaten. I hated to pass them, with their small, mad heads hanging down, but it was the only way to get to the dairy." One day, opening the door, she had seen an eyelid fall suddenly closed over an eye like a glass bead. "Now I dream that it is dead women who hang behind the door: and I imagine that one of them winks at me." Catching Ashlyme's astonished glance, she laughed and ran her hand along the arm of the chair. "Perhaps it never happened. Or not to me. Was I born in Soubridge, or have I been here all the time, in the plague zone? Here we are prone to a fevered imagination." She watched her hand a moment longer, moving on the arm of the chair, then seemed to fall asleep.

Ashlyme, relieved, immediately packed his chalks and folded his easel.

"I must go while it is still dark," he told the Fat Mam. She put her fingers to her lips. She held up one of the cards (he could not see what was on it, only the yellow reflection of the lamp), but did not answer otherwise. I will return, he pantomimed, tomorrow evening. As he passed her chair the dying woman whispered disconcertingly, "Yearning has its ghosts, Ashlyme. I painted such ghosts, as you well know. Not for my pleasure! It was an obligation. But all they want in the High City is trivia." She clutched his hand, her eyes still closed. "I don't want to go back there, Ashlyme, and they wouldn't have me if I did. I belong to the plague zone now."

The fortune-teller let him out into the street. The cat rubbed his legs. As he made off he heard something heavy falling down in an upper room, and a confused, ravaged voice calling, "Help me! Help me!"

He continued to visit the Rue Serpolet once or twice a week. He would have gone more frequently, but he had other commissions. An inexplicable lethargy gripped him: while he still had access to the dying woman, he found it hard to finalize his plans for her rescue. Still, the portrait progressed. In exchange for his preliminary sketches and caricatures, which had delighted her with their cruelty, she gave him some small canvases of her own. He was embarrassed. He was, he protested, only a journeyman. She coughed warningly. "I would be honored to take them," he said. He came no closer to understanding her relationship with the fortune-teller, who was now seen only rarely at her yellow booth in the Artists Quarter, and spent her time instead laundering bloody handkerchiefs, preparing meals which Audsley King allowed to cool uneaten, and endlessly turning over the cards.

The cards! The pictures on them glowed like crude stained glass, like a window on some other world, some escape. That the fortune-teller saw them so was plain. But Audsley King looked on expressionlessly, as before. She was using them, he thought, for something else, some more complex self-deception.

All his visits were made via the Gabelline Stairs. There was a considerable volume of traffic there during the plague months. Ashlyme made an oddly proper little figure among the poets and poseurs, the princelings, politicians, and popularists who might be found ascending or descending them at dawn and dusk. But his peculiar red coxcomb and wedge-shaped head gave him away as one of them. One morning just before dawn he encountered two drunken youths on the stairs where they went round behind Agden Fincher's famous pie shop. They were a rough-looking pair with scabby hands and hair of a dirty yellow color chopped to a stubble on their big round heads. They wore outlandish clothes which were covered with food stains and worse.

When he first saw them they were sitting on each side of the stairs and throwing a bruised melon back and forth between them. They were singing tunelessly:

"We are the Beezley brothers.
Ousted out of Birmingham and Wolverhampton,
Lords of the Left-Hand Brain,
The shadows of odd doings follows us through the
    night. . . ."

But they soon stopped that.

"Give us yer blessing, Vicar!" they called. They staggered up to Ashlyme and fell at his feet, bowing their heads. He had no idea who they had mistaken him for. Perhaps they would have done it to anybody. One of them gripped his ankles with both hands, stared up at him, and vomited on his shoes. "Oops!" Ashlyme was disgusted. He ignored them and walked on, but they followed him, trying out of curiosity to prize his easel from under his arm. "You should be ashamed of yourselves," he told them fiercely, trying to avoid their great sheepish blue eyes; they groaned and nodded. They accompanied him in this fashion about a hundred steps upward, winking conspiratorially when they thought he wasn't looking. Then they seemed to remember something else.

"Fincher's!" they shouted.

They began to pelt each other furiously with fruit and meat.

"Fincher, make us a pie!"

They tottered off, falling down and knocking on doors at random.

Ashlyme quickened his pace. The reek of squashed fruit followed him all the way up to the High City, where his shoes attracted some comment.

Who were these drunken brothers? It is not certain. They owned the city, or so they claimed. They had come upon it, they said, during the course of a mysterious journey. (Sometimes they claimed to have created it, in one day, from nothing but the dust which blows through the low hills of Monar. Millennia had passed since then, they explained.) At first they appeared in a quite different form: two figures materializing once or twice a decade in the sky above the Atteline Plaza of the city, huge and unrealistic like lobsters in their scarlet armor, staring down in an interested fashion. Mounted on vast white horses, they moved through the dark air like a constellation, fading away over a period of hours.

Now they lived in the High City with a Mingulay dwarf called the "Grand Cairo." They were trying to become human.

"This is a game to them, or seems to be," wrote Ashlyme in his diary, "a curious and violent one. Not a night passes without them becoming drunk. They hang about all day in the pissoir of some wine shop, carving their initials in the plaster on the walls, and after dark race along the Margarethestrasse, stuffing themselves with noodles and pies which they vomit up all over the steps of the Mausoleum of Cecilia Metalla at midnight."

Were they responsible for the city's present affliction? Ashlyme had always blamed them. "If they really are the landlords of the city," he wrote, "they are unreliable ones, with their 'Chinese take-away' and their atrocious argot."

While the Beezley brothers wrestled with their new humanity, the plague was lapping at the foot of the High City like a lake. An air of inexplicable dereliction spread across the entire Artists Quarter. The churchyards were full of rank marguerites, the streets plastered with torn political posters. Dull ironic laughter issued from the Bistro Californium and the Luitpold Café. In the mornings old women stared with expressions of intense intelligence into the windows of pie shops along the Via Gellia in the rain. While, up in the High City and all down the hill below Alves, dismayed servants were pulled across the roads by dogs like wolves on jeweled leashes. These were the secret agents of the Beezley brothers. "Everyone knows them," Ashlyme told his journal. "They pretend to be harassed and have receding hair, pretend to be exercising these gigantic dogs. On whom are they spying? To whom do they report? Accounts differ. Some say the brothers, some their dwarf. Now that the Beezleys are down among us, nothing is reliable."

Other police enforced the quarantine of the affected area. They were strangely apathetic and unpredictable. For a month no one would see them; suddenly they would put on smart black uniforms and arrest anyone trying to leave the zone, taking them away to undergo "tests." People detained in this way were released erratically and under no obvious system.

"I cannot take them seriously," Ashlyme wrote. "Are they police at all?"

They were. The next time he went to see Audsley King they stopped him at the foot of the Gabelline Stairs. It was a new policy. The plague zone was closed to him.

He went to see Emmet Buffeau instead. Buffeau lived at the top of an old house at Alves, halfway up the famous hill (the summit of which had interfered with many of his most radical and innovatory observations). Alves was a curious place. It was a windy salient or polyp of the High City flung out into the Low, partaking of the character of both. While its streets were wider than those of the Artists Quarter, they were no less shabby. Strange old towers rose from a wooded slope clasped in a curved arm of the derelict pleasure canal. They were uninhabited now. About their feet clustered the peeling villas of a vanished middle class, all plaster moldings, tottering porticoes, and drains smelling of cats. Ashlyme trudged up the hill. A bell clanged high up in a house; a face moved at a window. The wind whirled the dust and dead leaves round him.

While he waited for the astronomer to open his door, he thought ruefully of Audsley King's most popular watercolor, "On the Bridge at New Man's Staithe."

In this view of Alves a honey-colored light seems to rise from the glassy waters of the abandoned canal and enfold the hill behind, giving its eccentric architecture a mysterious familiarity, like buildings seen in a dream. The towers, their pastel colors thickened romantically, glow like stained glass.

Ashlyme smiled. A print of this picture hung in every salon in the High City. The question most frequently asked about it was: "This unmoving figure at the parapet of the bridge, is it male or female?" Audsley King would answer: "I did not intend you to know." She had painted it during a love affair sixteen years before. She now disowned its dreamy lights and sentimentality. "It is untruthful," she complained. "Yet they love it so!"

Emmet Buffeau put his head round the door and blinked. "Come in, come in!" he said.

He was tall and thin and his clothes made his arms and legs seem ill-fitting, of awkward or unequal length. They were the clothes, he imagined, that would set a doctor of astronomy apart from an amateur. He gave an impression of clumsiness, though he never actually knocked things over. His researches, which had something to do with the moon, were regarded with derision in the High City, but he did not suspect this. When he thought no one was watching him, his face relaxed into deep folds like a crumpled bag.

"Come in!"

He took Ashlyme's hand as if he had never met him before and, under the impression that he had been sent from some committee to explore the funding of a new telescope, led him up the stairs. He had, he explained, given up hope of ever getting money for his experiments. He did not blame the High City for this. Every six months he went to the patent office and was turned away.

"I wait for an hour, perhaps two, on the benches with all the others."

Up the stairs went Ashlyme behind him, listening to this monologue float down, unable to find any opportunity to speak and hardly knowing what to say anyway. There were pockets of dust in the corners of the landings.

"I understand the needs of the bureaucracy," Buffeau said. He understood its inertia. What could he do but maintain a philosophical attitude? "Still, they have sent you. That's something!"

He laughed.

He lived in a kind of penthouse, much of which he had built himself. It was cold there even in summer. In one room he cooked his food and slept; it was tidy, but a stale smell hung in the air about the low iron bed and the homemade washstand. He ground his lenses in another smaller room. Little pieces of colored glass like the petals of anemones littered a table, some set in complex frames made of a whitish metal. The astronomical charts had peeled that morning from one wall and lay in folds at its foot. (Moldy patterns in the plaster suggested that another universe had been hidden behind them.) "It's the damp," apologized Buffeau. He showed Ashlyme around like a tourist in the Margarethestrasse. "This is my 'exterior brain,'" he said. "I call it that. I can refer to it at any time. It's more than a library." He indicated an ordinary set of shelves on which were arranged reference books and instruments, models of telescopes, and bits of paper with technical drawings on them.

The adjoining room, where he spent most of his time, was a flimsy structure like a greenhouse, with a complicated system of ratchets and rods that enabled him to lift its roof and poke out his telescopes. It was composed of odd panes of glass, some colored, some milky; they were cracked and of different sizes.

"This is the observatory itself. From here I can see twenty miles in any direction."

Ashlyme looked out. A quarter of the sky was obscured by the bulk of Alves, with the cracked, threatening copper dome of an old palace askew on it like a crown. From the other side he could look down across the pleasure canal at the famous graves on Allman's Heath. "It was built to my own design, ten years ago," said Buffeau. It was full of contraptions. As Ashlyme moved from one to another, pretending not to have seen them before, Buffeau sat on a stool. He couldn't sit still. He hopped to his feet to explain something—"These are the plans for the new device"—and sat down again. He was like an exhibit himself in the odd light.

One of the contraptions was a maze of copper tubing into which Buffeau had let two or three eyepieces, apparently at random. Ashlyme bent to look through one of them. All he saw was a sad reticulated grayness and, suspended indistinctly against it in the distance, something like a chrysalis or cocoon, spinning at the end of its thread. Buffeau smiled shyly. "Success is slow to come with that one," he admitted. "You'd agree it had vast potential, though?" He went on to explain his experimental method, but soon saw that Ashlyme didn't understand. He left the observatory for a moment and came back with a tray. "Would you like some wine? Some of these sardines?" Thankfully, Ashlyme sat down and took some. They ate in silence. When he had finished Ashlyme rubbed his hands over his face.

"Buffeau," he said. "You know it's me, not some clerk from the patent office. It's Ashlyme. I've seen all this a hundred times before."

"Pardon?" Buffeau stared at him, his expression changing slowly. "I suppose you have," he said thoughtfully. He sighed. "I suppose I knew it all along, really. I'm sorry old chap."

"They've closed the plague zone," said Ashlyme. "What are we going to do?"

Buffeau looked bleakly round the observatory. "You wake from one nightmare into the next," he told himself in a quiet voice. He inspected the palm of his hand as if it were his whole life. "I'm sorry, this fish is awful. Leave it if you like." Suddenly he dropped his plate on the floor with a clatter, laughed, and jumped to his feet. Sponged of its lines, his face seemed much younger. "We must lay new plans, then!" he exclaimed. He touched Ashlyme's arm. "Come on, Ashlyme, it cheers me up just to see you!"

He had an idea already, he continued. They would wade across the pleasure canal at the foot of the hill. It was quite shallow. "You can see the bottom quite clearly on a sunny day." After that they could sneak across the graveyard at Allman's Heath; the Artists Quarter was barely three hundred yards away.

Ashlyme wiped the condensation off a pane of glass and stared at the dark loop of water, the jumble of roofs to the west, the leaning gravestones that filled the Heath between. (Had Audsley King set up her easel among them to paint "On the Bridge at New Man's Staithe," anemones and sol d'or burning at her feet? Now it was full of briers and plaster dust blown in from the aimless renovations on Endingall Street and deMonfried Square.) "We could do it easily," he heard himself agree.

Buffeau went over and opened a cupboard. Out fell what looked like a bundle of rags, wrapped in something more solid.

"Don't look for a moment," he said.

Ashlyme was forced to smile. He closed his eyes, ran his tongue round the inside of his mouth to dislodge a piece of sardine. When he opened his eyes again he saw Buffeau standing there wearing a kind of varnished rubber mask. It covered his head completely and resembled the stripped and polished skull of a horse, two pomegranates set in the empty sockets to simulate eyes. It was ludicrous. Buffeau had taken off his clothes and wound strips of green swaddling round his body. His arms and legs were like sticks, his ribcage huge. Two great branched feathery horns came up out of the forehead of the mask. He did not look human. "They're rather well done, aren't they?" he said, his voice muffled by the rubber which was forced down over his nose. "Don't you want to look at yours?" He had another mask in his outstretched hand.

Ashlyme backed away. "No," he said. "I don't want to see it. Why are you dressed like that?"

"I thought it made me look like a beggar. No one will recognize us if we wear these." He pounced on Ashlyme and took him by the shoulders. He whirled him round and round in a clumsy dance. "What an idea!" he crowed. "What a success!"

Ashlyme was helpless. The skull of the horse was thrust into his face. It was hard to believe that Buffeau's familiar features were somewhere beneath it. He was as frightened by the strength of the astronomer's thin arms as he was by the sound of breath sobbing in and out of the mask. Then he began to laugh despite himself.

"Well done, Buffeau!"

Buffeau, encouraged, sang a mawkish but lively popular song. They finished the bottle of wine and even the sardines. The sun set. Crowing and singing, they pranced about the observatory, bumping into things and falling down, until they were exhausted.

Later, with the proper fall of night, the observatory became cold and uninhabitable; but the two men sat on, talking at first, then contemplating their plan in a companionable silence. They discussed the future. Buffeau would move out of Alves and into the High City, where he believed his work would be better appreciated; Ashlyme would share his studio with Audsley King and they would do great work together. The flimsy structure of the greenhouse creaked around them as the wind rose. Damp air blew through the cracked panes, giving Ashlyme the impression of motion, of racing travel through some ramshackle but benign dimension. Where would they end up? He smiled over at Buffeau. The astronomer's head had sunk onto his chest; he had fallen asleep with his mouth open and begun to snore. Turned down, the lamps emitted a queer crepuscular light. Ashlyme got his cloak and folded it about him. It was too late to go home. Besides, he felt somehow responsible for the astronomer, who looked even more honest asleep than he did awake. He wandered about for a while, squinting into the eyepieces of the waiting telescopes. Then he sat down and dozed. Once or twice he woke up suddenly, thinking about the pile of clothes and masks on the floor.

For a week he felt debauched and bilious, uninclined to commit himself. Were the quarantine police watching his movements? Was Emmet Buffeau a broken reed? "The plague," he wrote in his diary, "permeates all our decisions, like a fog." For the most part he stayed in his studio, watching morosely as the unseasonable rain swept across the Low

City and lashed the fronts of the houses at Mynned. "This summer is a travesty," he wrote. And, on finding water among his belongings in the attic, "I am appalled, but it is my own fault. I have not repaired the roof." Neither had he repaired his opinion of the High City art cliques. "Is anything worthwhile being done? In short, no: up here it is all dinner arrangements and affairs. Rack has had the sets for 'Die Traumunden Knaben' for a month now, yet there have been no auditions, no readings. He wishes, he says, 'to consult the artist'; but he will never go to the Low City."

He could not work on the portrait of Audsley King. Instead he began framing the pictures she had given him. He discovered with delight the early landscape 'A Conflagration This Wednesday at Lowth,' and what appeared to be an incomplete gouache of the notorious 'Self-Portrait Half-Clothed,' in which the artist is seen peering slyly into a mirror, her long hands touching her own private parts. He hung the paintings in different places to find the best light and stood in front of them for long periods, thrilled by the stacked planes of the landscapes, the disquieting eros of her inner world.

At last an oblique sunshine broke through the clouds above the city and filled it with a shifting, fitful brightness. There was a rush to the banks of the pleasure canal. The High City emptied itself onto Lime Walk and the Terrace of the Fallen Leaves, and there, in audacious proximity to the plague zone, took the sun.

Little iron tables were set up, and the women drank tea out of porcelain "lucid as a baby's ear," while those poets who had escaped exile in the Californium and the Luitpold Café recited in musical voices. Everyone had a theory about the plague. Everyone had it from a reliable source. Most agreed it would never reach the High City. Imagine the scene! The women had on their muslin dresses. The men wore swords and meal-colored cloaks copied carefully from

those fashionable among Low City mohocks two or three
centuries before. A wet silvery light fell delicately on the
white bridges, limning the afternoon curve of the canal and
perfectly disguising its shabbiness. Everyone enjoyed themselves thoroughly, while down below, among the ragwort
on the towpath, writhed the thousand-and-one black-and-
yellow caterpillars of the cinnabar moth, some fat and in-
dustrious, rearing up their ugly blunt heads, others thin and
scruffy and torpid. The Beezley brothers ate them and were
sick.

Ashlyme, who had been out buying mastic, wandered
onto the Terrace of the Fallen Leaves and could not find
his way off again. The crowds confused him. He ran into
Paulinus Rack, who was sitting at a table with Livio Fognet
the lithographer and their patron the Marchioness "L." A
shy young novelist stood behind the Marchioness's chair,
admiring the famous curve of her upper arm. They were all
delighted to see Ashlyme. What a stranger he was! "Has
the plague lifted, then?" he said, staring in puzzlement about
him. It was the only reason he could think of for a celebration. They were amused. Had he never heard of sunshine? He accepted a cup of tea the Marchioness had poured
especially for him, but declined to watch the antics of the
Beezley brothers down on the canal bank. He could not
think of them, he explained, as a sideshow.

"Aren't you being a little naive, old chap?" said Livio
Fognet. He winked at the Marchioness's novelist.

"After all," chided the Marchioness, "we must think of
them as something!" She laughed shrilly, and then seemed
to lose her confidence. "Mustn't we?"

A bemused silence followed. After a minute or so her
novelist said, "I don't think Rack himself could have put it
better." He blushed. He was saved by a general movement
toward the railings. A murmur of laughter went up and down
the terrace. "Oh, do look, Paulinus!" cried the Marchioness.

"One of them has fallen in, right up to the knees!"

Rack gave her a mechanical glance and a twist of his fat lips. He shrugged. "My dear Marchioness," he said, and moved his chair closer to Ashlyme's. He could create a little eddy of intimacy in any crowd. We, he was able to suggest with a touch of one plump hand, have nothing in common with these people. Why are we here at all? It was a flattering device, and he owed to it much of his social and financial success. "Fognet's a buffoon, I'm afraid," he murmured, leaning forward a little. "And the Marchioness a parasite. I wish we could have met under better circumstances."

"But I love the Marchioness," said Ashlyme. "Don't you?"

Rack looked at him uncertainly. "You surprise me." He laughed. He raised his voice. "By the way," he said. "How *is* Audsley King?"

"Oh, yes," said the Marchioness plaintively. "We are all appalled by her situation."

The Beezley brothers, egged on by the laughter from above, linked arms and jumped into the canal together, showering the tables along the terrace with bright drops of spray. They had found a spot where the water was deeper. It surged and bubbled; then their great red faces appeared, puffing and blowing, above its greenish surface. "Gor!" they said. "It i'n' half cold!" They coughed and spat, they shook their heads about and stuck their fingers in their ears to get the water out. The little screams of the women encouraged them to thrash about (it could hardly be called swimming), to blow bubbles, and to push one another under. Presently they dragged themselves out, water gushing out of their trouser legs and running down the towpath. They grinned stupidly upward, too exhausted now to go back in for their shoes.

Ashlyme was enraged by this display. "Audsley King is coughing her left lung up, Marchioness," he said bitterly.

"She is dying, if you want to know. What will you do about that?" He laughed. "I do not see you much abroad in the plague zone!"

The Marchioness blinked into her teacup. It seemed for a moment that she would not answer. Finally she said. "You judge people by unrealistic standards, Master Ashlyme. That is why your portraits are so cruel." She looked thoughtfully at the tea leaves, then got to her feet and took the arm of her novelist. "Though I daresay we are as stupid as you make us appear." She adjusted her dove-gray gloves. "I hope you'll tell Audsley King that we are still her friends," she said. And she went away between the surrounding tables, exchanging a word here and there with people she knew. Once or twice the young novelist looked angrily back at Ashlyme, but she touched his shoulder in a placatory way, and soon they were lost to view.

Paulinus Rack bit his lip. "Damn!" he said. "I shall have to pay for that later." He stared across the canal. "You'll find you've carried this attitude too far."

"What are you going to do when the plague reaches the High City, Rack?" asked Ashlyme with some contempt.

Rack ignored him. "Your work may be less fashionable in future. If I were you I would be prepared for that. Never insult a paying customer." He made a dismissive gesture. "You cannot save Audsley King anyway," he said.

Ashlyme was furious. He grabbed at Rack's arm. Rack looked frightened and pulled it away. Ashlyme caught him by the fingers instead. He twisted them. "What do you know?" he jeered. "I'll have her out of the plague zone within the week." Rack only curled his lip. He had made no attempt to free his fingers, so Ashlyme twisted them harder. "What do you say to that?" He wanted to see Rack wince, or hear him apologize; but nothing like that happened. They sat there for some time, looking at one another defiantly. Livio Fognet, who did not seem to understand the situation, winked and grinned impartially at them. It started to rain. The High City opened its umbrella and took itself off to Mynned, while the Beezley brothers put their arms over their heads to protect themselves from the rain and, groaning, watched their shoes float away toward Alves. Ashlyme let Rack's fingers go. "Within the week," he repeated.

"I'll just go and have a word with Angina Desformes," said Livio Fognet.

"There is a certain time of the afternoon," said Audsley King, "when everything seems repellent to me."

The city was unseasonably dank again, the air chilly and lifeless. Tarot cards were scattered across the floor of the studio as if someone had slung them there in a fit of rage. Audsley King lay in a nest of brocade pillows on the faded sofa, her thin body propped up on one elbow. On the easel in front of her she had propped a grotesque little charcoal sketch in which a conductor, beating time with extravagant sweeps of the baton, cut off the heads of the poppies which made up his orchestra. It was full of overt violence, quite unlike her usual work. It was unfinished, and she regarded it with flushed features and angry, frustrated gestures. In her preoccupation she had allowed the studio fire to burn down; but she did not seem to feel the cold. This wasn't a good sign.

Ashlyme stood awkwardly in the middle of the room. He felt shy, guilty, inadequate, not so much in the knowledge of the betrayal he had come to effect, as in his inability thereby to make any real change in her circumstance. He had never before been so aware of the bareness of the gray floorboards, the impermanent air of the canvases piled in the corners, the age and condition of the furniture. He opened his mouth to say, "In the High City they would take more care of you," but thought better of it. Instead he studied the two new paintings that hung unframed on the wall. Both were of Fat Mam Etteilla, and showed her crouching on the floor, shuffling the cards. Under one of them the artist had written in a slanting hand, "THE DOOR INTO THE OPEN!" They were hurried and careless, like the cartoon on the easel, as if she had lost faith in her technique—or patience with the very medium.

"You shouldn't work so hard," he said.

She was amused.

"Work? This is nothing." She dabbed at the sketch, looked disgustedly at the resulting line, and smeared it with her long thumb. "When I lived in the midlands," she said, "I would paint from six in the morning until it grew dark."

She laughed.

"'Six in the morning, and chrome yellow is back in nature!' Do you know that quotation? My eyes never grew tired. The plowland stretched away like a dark dream, covered in mist. Rooks creaked above it, circling the elms. My husband—"

She stopped. Her mouth curved in regret, and then in self-contempt.

"What a masterpiece this is!"

She struck the canvas so hard that her charcoal broke. The easel tottered, folded itself up, and fell over with a clatter.

"The field of poppies is the field you have sown!" she cried, looking vaguely into the air in front of her. "It is like an orchestra in which the players take no notice of their conductor. Am I raving?"

Suddenly she collapsed among the pillows and blood poured out of her mouth. It ran along her arm and began to soak into the brocade. She stared helplessly down at herself.

"My husband was an artist too. He was far better than I am. Shall I show you?" She tried to get up, slumped back, dabbed at herself with a handkerchief. "Nothing of his is left, of course." Her eyes focused on Ashlyme. Tears poured out of them. "No, I am quite all right, thank you."

Ashlyme was dismayed. She had never been married. (Before moving to the city she had lived, as far as he knew, with her parents. This had been several years ago, and no paintings survived from the period.) The hemorrhage had brought to the surface in this inexplicable delusion some deeply buried internal drama. She clutched his wrist and pulled him close to her. Embarrassed, he stared into the thin face, white as a gardenia, with its harshly cut features and strange voracious lines about the mouth. She whispered something more, but in the middle of a sentence fell asleep. After a moment he detached himself gently from her grip and, walking like a man in a dream, went out into the passage.

"Come on, Buffeau," he said.

It had been their intention to dose Audsely King with laudanum, although neither of them, frankly, had been clear how this might be done. She ate so little. They had discussed putting it in a glass of wine. "But how to make sure she drinks it?" The drug now seemed unnecessary, but Buffeau was an inflexible conspirator and insisted she have it anyway. In the event, he did not give her enough: as the stuff touched her tongue she moaned and moved her head with the practiced obstinacy of the invalid (who fears that every surrender to sleep might be the last), so that most of the dose trickled down her cheek. The little she swallowed, though, had an eerie effect. After a moment she sat bolt upright, and with her eyes firmly closed, said clearly:

" '*Les mortes, les pauvre mortes, ont de grand doleurs.*' Michael?"

Buffeau gave a tremendous guilty leap and spilled the remainder of the draft on the floor.

"What?" he shouted. "Are we discovered already?"

Ashlyme, who could see that the woman was only talking in her sleep, tried to pull him away from her. He resisted stubbornly, plucking at Ashlyme's clothes and hair.

"The noise!" appealed Ashlyme in an urgent whisper. "You'll wake her, you madman!"

They tottered about on the bare boards in the failing light, panting, hissing, pushing at one another, while the thick smell of the drug rose up all round them.

"She has not taken it!"

"Nevertheless!"

Audsley King groaned suddenly, as if seeking their attention, and subsided into the pillows. They stopped struggling and watched her warily. Her mouth fell open. She began to snore.

They had a handcart waiting below in the Rue Serpolet, and their plan was to carry her downstairs in an old linen sheet belonging to Buffeau. Her limbs were lax and uncooperative, and she was heavier than her wasted appearance had led Ashlyme to suspect. "Hurry!" A fierce heat seemed to radiate from her skin. Upside down, her face—with its bluish hollows and trickle of dried blood—looked accusatory, ironical, amused. They muddled it, and could not get her off the sofa and onto the sheet. Ashlyme would not continue. "We've killed her!" he said. The whole idea was mad. He would have nothing more to do with it. In the end Buffeau had to lift her onto the sheet while Ashlyme stood by with a blunted upholstery needle, ready to sew her in with long, loose stitches.

"Now the disguises. Be quick!"

Buffeau took his clothes off in a corner. As he hopped from one foot to the other on the cold floor, trying to conceal himself, a strong smell of camphor wafted from him. Ashlyme, embarrassed by his friend's modesty, turned over the scattered tarot cards or glanced out of the window at the yellowish underbelly of the clouds above the Rue Serpolet.

He began to believe that the scheme might succeed after all. He would offer Audsley King space in his own studio while she reorganized her life. He would get her away from Rack and the Marchioness "L": there would be other art dealers, other patrons only too willing to take her on. He tapped his fingers on the windowsill. "Hurry," he urged Buffeau. "Even now the fortune-teller may be returning."

Buffeau, swaddled at last in his disagreeable bandages, pulled the rubber mask over his head and turned to face into the room.

He asked, "Is it on straight?" which Ashlyme heard as a sepulchral and threatening, "Iv id om fdrade?" Yellow light, reflected from the clouds outside, splashed down one side of the mask. It looked like a horse's head, newly scraped to the bone in a knacker's yard and decked with green paper ribbons for some festival. But its horns and eyes belonged to nothing on earth. The astronomer patted it with one cupped hand, like a woman adjusting a hat, and came toward Ashlyme, who shuddered and backed away, saying:

"Must I wear such an awful thing?"

Buffeau laughed. "Yours isn't half so striking. Here—!"

Ashlyme accepted the damp and sweaty rubber with distaste. He forced it quickly down over his face so as not to give himself time to think, and was at once unable to breathe. Nauseated by its smell, his nose squashed over to one side, his left eye covered, he struggled to tear it off, but found the astronomer's hands forcing it back on. "I need no help! Leave me alone!" He was disgusted with himself as much as with Buffeau. This fetid confinement, more than anything else, made the plan unbearable. His eyes were streaming. When he could see again he glared resentfully at Buffeau's swathed, sticklike limbs.

"I won't be bandaged up like that, whatever you say!"

Buffeau shrugged.

"Suit yourself, then."

The lower stairs of the house were bathed in a dim yellow light and strewn with the lathe and plaster dislodged daily by the landlord's workmen. Abandoned building materials lay about on each landing. Ashlyme and the astronomer picked their way down through this litter, Audsley King slung between them like a stolen carpet. (While behind their doors the other occupants of the house ignored the furtive thudding on the stairs, and spoke in the desultory, argumentative tones of the plague zone, asking one another if it meant to rain, or what they would get from the butcher tomorrow.)

Audsley King shook her head restively and groaned. "I cannot have those great lilies in here," she said in a low, reasonable voice. "You know how hard it is to get my breath." She trembled once or twice and was still.

Ashlyme and Buffeau redoubled their efforts. She seemed to have grown heavier with every step, numbing their arms and slipping out of their aching fingers. They weren't used to the work, and bickered over it like two old men: if Buffeau was not pulling forward too hard, then Ashlyme was hanging back. Neither dared raise his voice to the other but, trammeled in his rancid helmet, could only curse the thick hiss of his own breath in his ears and wish himself back in the High City. Their feet scraped and slithered on the stairs.

"Don't *pull!*"

"If only you would stop pushing like that!"

Without warning, Audsley King, dreaming perhaps, drew her knees up to her chin, and the sheet contracted like a huge ghostly chrysalis in the gloom. Ashlyme lost his grip on her shoulders. She slipped forward, knocked Buffeau off his feet, and tumbled down the stairs after him, bumping and groaning on every step, to fetch up with a hollow thud among the bags of sand and lime on a landing not far below.

"Buffeau!" appealed Ashlyme. "Be more careful!"

Buffeau stared up at him with hatred, his absurd barrel chest heaving beneath its rags. The sheet writhed briefly;

snores came from it. They approached it cautiously.

"Where am I?" said Audsley King.

She had regained consciousness, and obviously believed herself to be alone.

"Am I in hell? Oh, nothing will ever console me for the ghastliness of this condition!"

It was the voice of someone who wakes in a bare room in an unknown city, stares dully at the washstand and the disordered bed, and having pulled open every empty drawer, turns at last to the window and the empty streets below, only to discover she has lived here all her life.

"Another hemorrhage. If only I could die."

She considered this, then forgot it.

"My father said, 'Why draw this filth?'" she went on. "'If you abuse your talents you will lose them. They will be taken from you if you draw filth.' It's so dark in here. I didn't want to go to bed so soon."

There was a small sob. She struggled a little, as if to test the limits of her confinement.

She stiffened.

A piercing shriek issued from the sheet.

Ashlyme tried to get hold of her feet, but she tore herself out of his grasp and began to roll back and forth across the landing, knocking into the walls and shouting, "I am not dead! I am not dead!"

At this, doors flew open up and down the stairs and out came her neighbors to complain about the noise. A few ducked back at once when they saw what was happening; but several of them, mainly women, exchanged puzzled if ironical nods and settled down to watch. Emmet Buffeau, who had rehearsed such an eventuality, explained to anyone who would listen: "Official business. Quarantine police. Keep back!" This was so manifestly ridiculous that he was ignored (although in the melee that was to develop later it did him more harm than good).

Audsley King, meanwhile, had ripped the sheet open

along Ashlyme's rough seam and thrust one of her long, powerful hands through the gap to clutch desperately at the air. By now she was so frightened that she had started to cough again in a series of deep, destructive spasms between which she could only retch and gasp. A red bloom appeared at the upper end of the sheet and spread rapidly. Ashlyme lifted her into a sitting position. "Please be calm," he begged. The convulsions decreased a little. He was ready to confess the whole sordid business to her, but he did not know where to begin. Gently, he freed her head and arms from the sheet. The women crowded forward, silent, uncertain, no longer amused; they groaned angrily at the sight of her white cheeks and bloody lips. She blinked up at them. Her hands were hot; she took one of Ashlyme's between them.

"I beg of you whoever you are to get me out of this shroud," she said.

Suddenly she caught sight of the thing he had over his head. She began to scream again, flailing her arms and begging him not to hurt her.

This was too much for the women, who advanced on Ashlyme jeering and rolling up their sleeves. Emmet Buffeau stepped in front of them, making gestures he imagined to be placatory. He took several nasty knocks about the head and chest and was pushed into a pile of sand, where he lay jerking his long legs ineffectually and repeating, "Official police, official police."

Audsley King thrust Ashlyme away. "Fish into man: man into fish!" she cried, in a thick midland accent—remembering perhaps some solstitial bonfire, some girlhood ritual in the heavy plowland. "Murderer!"

Ashlyme fell back astonished.

A fish?

He touched the mask with his fingers. It was the head of a trout, to which someone had added thick rubbery lips and a ludicrous crest of spines. He clapped his hands to his head and, reeling about in disgust, tried vainly to pull the mask off. Its smell grew horrifying. Why had he conspired to make himself so absurd? He could think now only of escaping. Audsley King would have to be abandoned. In the High City he would be a laughing stock. He threw himself at the women, who were punching and kicking Buffeau with a kind of dazed, preoccupied savagery, and dragged the astronomer away from them.

"Bitten off more than you can swallow, eh?" they sneered. "Let's have them headpieces off and see who you really are!"

Having won the day, though, they made no attempt to carry out this threat. One of them attended to Audsley King, while the rest stood arms akimbo, sniffing defiantly, or tugged nervous fingers through their ruffled hair.

Ashlyme, weeping with shame and anger, ran down the stairs and into the street, where rain had begun to pour from the yellow undersides of the clouds, spattering the dusty chestnut trees and making a greasy cement out of the plaster dust and fallen leaves on the pavement. Buffeau staggered out after him confused and bleeding, his rags coming un-wrapped and his dreadful headdress knocked askew. Seeing that they were not pursued, they leaned against the handcart. "Those wretched women," panted the astronomer. "They will always ruin your plans." Ashlyme stared speechlessly at him for a moment, then walked off.

The rain fell.

Buffeau called, "What about the handcart? Ashlyme?"

Fat Mam Etteilla trudged into sight, her head down into the rain.

Buffeau gave a start of surprise, grabbed the handles of the cart, and ran erratically down the Rue Serpolet with it until one of its wheels came off. It mounted the curb and fell on its side. Buffeau looked round in panic, as if he had lost his bearings, then made off with long strides into the gathering darkness between two buildings, calling, "Ashlyme? Ashlyme?" The fortune-teller watched from the doorstep of Audsley King's house. Her eyes were noncommittal; her arms were full of greengrocery. She shrugged and entered the house. A few moments afterward a great wail went up, doors were banged, the lights came on in Audsley King's studio, and there was a great deal of coming and going between floors.

Ashlyme, who had been hiding from Buffeau in a wet doorway, waited until the commotion had died down and then went home, soaked.

Later he stared into the mirror above his washstand, hardly seeing the lugubrious, blubbery-lipped totem that stared back out at him, its eyes popping solemnly and its loose scales dropping into the sink. All the way back he had dreaded trying to remove it; but it came off quite easily in the end.

The period that followed was quiet and nerve-racking. He woke guiltily from every sleep. In the middle of stretching a canvas or doing his housework he would recall some incident of the debacle and be overwhelmed by a wave of horror and shame. He could not turn his clients away when they came to pose, yet dreaded every knock on the door in case it was the quarantine police or—worse still—some message full of contempt from Audsley King, delivered by the avenging fortune-teller. But no summons came from either quarter.

"I hear nothing from Emmet Buffeau," he wrote in his diary. And went on, perhaps unfairly. "Why should I seek him out? The whole farrago was his fault." He reminded himself in the same breath, "I must avoid Rack and his clique. How can I face them now, with their sneers and insinuations?"

In fact, he had no difficulty. Ironically enough, his en-

counter with them on the Terrace of the Fallen Leaves had
only increased his standing in the High City. Rumors of the
failed rescue attempt—which, when they filtered up to
Mynned from the exiles in the Bistro Californium and the
Luitpold Café, were mercifully vague—merely added to
his new romantic stature. He was popular in the salons. The
Marchioness called on him, with a new novelist. He was
forced for the first time in his career to turn away commissions. The two or three portraits he completed at this
time tended to be kinder than usual. This embarrassed him,
and rather disappointed his clients. For once no one wanted
an Ashlyme they could live with. They craved his bad opinion. He was their conscience. Not that he could compete
with the plague, or the Beezley brothers; and of the latter
he was soon writing:

"In the salons we hear nothing but what clothes they
wear, what wine shop they frequent this week, how they
have got pregnant some silly young *brodeuse* from the Pi-
azza of Inherited Tendencies. 'Will the Beezley brothers
dine at home tonight?' the women ask one another. 'Or will
they dine abroad?' They will eat like pigs in the pie shops
behind the Margarethestrasse. 'The Beezley brothers have
invented *Egg Foo Yung...!*'"

No one in the High City knew where they lived. They
were said to own two houses somewhere in the windy avenues between Haagsche Bosch and Montrouge. "Their
servants live on one side, and they and their dwarf (who
believes himself a king and is treated as such) on the other.
There is a high pastel tower lined with books, and a grave
beneath the pavement in which they have arranged a triple
sepulcher for themselves and the dwarf." Of the dwarf Ashlyme had little to record. "Nobody ever sees him. He is
pathologically violent and sensitive, so the story goes, and
spends all day banging on the walls to complain about the
noise the Beezley brothers are making. His secret police are

very active, especially along the edges of the plague zone. The whole city is nervous."

We can imagine how much of this anxiety was Ashlyme's own.

"What of Audsley King?" he wrote. "I see her plunged in a dream where all the faces are masks. Did she recognize my voice in the melee on that wretched staircase? I cannot go back there without knowing!"

But he did. He went to the house in the Rue Serpolet about nine days later, a dozen lilies waxen and heavy in the crook of his arm.

"How are you?"

"As you see me."

The room was cold. She lay on the sofa—thin; still; dazed-looking—wrapped in a fur coat with curiously huge sleeves. She spoke reluctantly of "thieves"; her eyes moved nervously every time a cart went past the house, and she made him go to the window to look. Bowls of anemones stood on every flat surface, as if she had begun to mourn herself. The flowers were purple and dark red, the colors of her disease; their necks were bent compliantly. She discussed small things: her domestic arrangements—"I am here in the studio all day now. It tires me so to have to move from room to room"—and her meals. ("I have a sudden dislike for fish!" she laughed. He studied her closely, but she was not laughing at him.) She had done no new work. Her easel was folded against the wall. She had done some cartoons, she said, but he could not see them, because they were no good. She had hung them for a day only. She would be glad to sit for him again. Life seemed so quiet; it was not empty, but very quiet.

"I have so much to think about!" she would say. "There is barely time in the day!"

As he left she was staring uneasily into the corners of the room. "The fortune-teller is very kind, but I miss the High City," she admitted.

He resumed his visits, recklessly using the Gabelline Stairs to get in and out of the Quarter. He began the portrait all over again, watching her helplessly: every day another layer of flesh melted away, deepening the bluish hollows underneath her cheekbones. Her face was constantly refining itself, seeking the exact expression of its underlying bone structure to be found in death. To occupy her (and, to an extent, himself) he told lies about Paulinus Rack, and invented the most outrageous affairs for the Marchioness "L." Livio Fognet he bankrupted. He lied without mercy. She was eager to believe anything. For the first time, he sensed, her courage had faltered, and she was sustained in her determination to remain only by her self-contempt, her appalling strength of will. This disappointed him obscurely.

Outside the studio the Low City deteriorated daily, its meaningless commerce and periods of stunned lethargy mimicking the full erosion of Audsley King's spirit. Shredded political posters flapped from the iron railings. Rain blew across the muddy grass. The horse-chestnut flowers guttered like gray wax candles. The plague cut off first Moon Street, then Thousand Suns Square, making peninsulas, then archipelagoes out of them; finally it engulfed each little island while its unsuspecting inhabitants were asleep. In the sodden churchyards and empty squares the police of the Beezley brothers stood about in small groups. Poets droned from the abandoned estaminets.

"Audsley King seems to observe all this from a dream," wrote Ashlyme. "Her expression is terrible: hungry, despairing, hopeful, all at once."

He could not release himself from a sense of guilt.

One afternoon, at her insistence, he lit a bonfire in the small garden at the rear of the house and carried her out to watch it.

"How nice this is," she said.

There was no wind. Within the tall brick walls—which,

with their mats of bramble, bladder senna and reddish ivy, dulled the sounds of construction coming from the buildings on either side—the air was sharp and rapturous, the light a curiously bleached lemon color. The smoke of Ashlyme's blaze, of which he was deeply proud and which he fed energetically with dead elder branches and sprays of yellow senna, hung motionless above the house, its scent remaining sharp and autumnal even when it mixed with the smoke of the builders' fires. Audsley King watched him affectionately, smiling a little at some recollection. But when he began to pull down living ivy, she chided, "Be careful Ashlyme that those tangled stems do not fasten themselves round your dreams. They will have their revenge." But it was plain that her own dreams concerned her, not his. "Let's burn the furniture instead. I shan't need it, soon."

He eyed her warily. He could not tell if she was teasing him. All day her mood had been changeable, demanding.

"Paint me!" she ordered suddenly. "I don't know how you can bear to waste this light!"

It was a long, strange afternoon.

The too-large collar of Audsley King's fur coat conspired with the bleached light to diminish and soften the mannishness of her features until she looked, as she stared into the fire, like a child staring out of a familiar window. Ashlyme, encouraged, worked steadily; he had never had so complaisant a model. Meanwhile Fat Mam Etteilla came and went, communicating a monolithic calm as she burned the household rubbish. Into the fire went old picture frames, Audsley King's bloodied handkerchiefs, a chair with one leg missing, a cardboard box which when it burst slowly open revealed a compressed mass of papers tied with old ribbon. She watched them all reduced to ashes, her agreeable face reddened by the heat, patches of sweat appearing under her arms. She was like a great patient horse, gazing with drooping underlip across an empty field.

(Ashlyme studied her covertly. Did she suspect him of the kidnap attempt? He thought not. But her opinions were invisible.)

Later, old women came out to sit on their balconies, looking up at the sky like animals about to be drowned. Fat Mam Etteilla fetched down her cards, laid them out on an old baize table, and predicted, "A good marriage, a bad end." The workmen next door brought down a wall, more by accident than design, and the old women, cackling appreciatively, watched the dust belly up into the air. The light shifted secretively a degree at a time, until it had left Ashlyme's work behind. Audsley King, anyway, had evaded him again: the heat of the fire had relaxed her narrow, angular face and softened the lines round her mouth. He was reluctant to change her pose, for the comfortable crackling of the fire had induced in him a hypnotic sense of time suspended, time retrieved; so he began a new charcoal study instead. After he had been scratching away at this for a few minutes, Audsley King said, "Before I came to the city I cut off my hair. It was the first of many fatally symbolic gestures."

She contemplated this statement as if trying to judge its completeness while Ashlyme, intrigued, looked at her sidelong and carefully said nothing.

"It was the autumn before I married," she went on. "The servants brought out all the rubbish which had accumulated in the house during the past year and burned it in the garden, just as we are doing here. Our parents looked on, while the children ran about cheering, or stared gravely into the red heart of the flames. We loved those autumn fires!"

She shook her head.

"How can I explain myself? I cut off my hair and threw it on the fire. Was it despair or intoxication? I was going to the city to begin a new life. I was going to be married. From now on I would paint what I saw, see everything I wished to see. Viriconium! How much it meant to me then!"

She laughed. She shrugged.

"I know what you are going to say. And yet . . . we were all going to be famous then—Ignace Retz the woodblock illustrator, elbowing his way down the Rue Montdampierre in his shabby black coat at lunchtime; Osgerby Practal, with nothing then to his name but his sudden drugged stupors and his craving for 'all human experience'; even Paulinus Rack. Oh, you may laugh, Ashlyme, but we took Paulinus Rack quite seriously then, going about his business in a donkey cart, with that sulfurous yellow cockatoo perched on his shoulder! He was thinner. He hadn't yet turned a whole generation of painters into tepid watercolorists and doomed consumptive aesthetes on behalf of the High City art collectors."

She made a sad defensive gesture.

"Once when I was ill he brought me a white kitten." She smiled. "Once," she said, "he tried to kill himself on the banks of the pleasure canal. He pressed a scarf soaked in ether to his face until his legs gave way, but was pulled out of the water before he could drown. We all rather admired him for that.

"Later I understood the weariness of this dream, and of the people who pursued it through the smoke in the Bistro Californium, the Antwerp Estaminet. Oh, we were all going to be famous then—Kristodulos, Astrid Gerstl, 'La Divinette.' But my husband contracted a howling syphilis and hanged himself one stifling afternoon in the back parlor of a herbalist's shop. He was twenty-three years old and had saved no money.

"I was too proud to go back to my mother. I was too determined. 'Your hair was not your own to cut,' she had written to me. 'It was mine. I had cared for it since you were born. What right had you to betray such a trust?' We spoke again only once before she died."

Finally she said:

"I regret none of this. Do you understand?" and was silent again. She closed her eyes. "Will someone build up the fire? I am cold."

For a long time nothing happened in the garden. Afternoon crept toward evening, the fire burned down; the fortune-teller somnolently addressed her cards. Ashlyme sketched the strange long hands of Audsley King. (Later he was to use them as the basis of the equivocal sequence "Studies of Some of My Friends"—fifty small oils on wood which bemuse us by their repetition of a single image differentiated only by minute changes in the background light.) Occasionally he glanced at her face. Her eyes were half-closed, mimicking the exhausted trance of the invalid, while from beneath the gray papery lids she judged his reaction to her little biographical fable. He had decided to hold his tongue. He would take the story away with him and hope its meaning eventually became clear.

"One July," she said suddenly, "storms came up from Radiopolis nine days in succession, and always at the same time in the evening. We sat in the summer house, my sisters and I, watching the damp soak into the colors of the dome which formed its roof." She spoke quickly and fractiously, as if she had pulled this memory across like a screen to hide something else. "In drier weather, these patterns, radiating from the keystone of the dome, turned powdery and faint—"

She broke off distractedly.

"My life is like a letter torn up twenty years ago," she said in a low, anguished voice. "I have thought about it so often that the original sense is lost."

The unfinished portrait attracted her attention. She got unsteadily to her feet and stumbled through the edges of the fire, the hem of her coat scattering charcoal and ashes. She took the canvas off the easel and stared intently at it. "Who is this?" she demanded. "What a travesty!" She laughed loudly and threw it in the fire. It lay there inertly in the middle of the flames, then, with a sudden dull whooshing sound, flared up white and orange. "Who is it, Ashlyme?" She whirled round and struck out at him, groaned with vertigo, fell against him, as hot and fragile as a bird. He grasped her wrists. "None of it will work now," she whispered. "How could you let me die here, Ashlyme?"

This was so unfair he could think of nothing to say. He blinked helplessly at the burning portrait.

Fat Mam Etteilla, accustomed to these brief and febrile rebellions, had got patiently to her feet. Now she spread her great capable arms in an elephantine gesture of comfort and tried to sweep Audsley King up in them. Audsley King, choking and weeping, avoided her with a fishlike twist. "Go back to your damned gutter!" she said. She caught sight of the tarot pack spread out on the fortune-teller's table. "These cards will never save me now. They smell of candles. They smell of old lust." She consigned them in handfuls to the flames, where they fluttered, blackened, and finally blazed like caged linnets in a house fire in the Rue Montdampierre.

"Where is the intercession that you promised?" wept Audsley King. "Where is the remission you foresaw?" And she darted away across the garden to crouch coughing desperately at the base of the wall.

Four or five of the cards, though charred at the edges, had escaped worse damage. Without quite knowing why, Ashlyme pulled them out of the fire and gave them back to the fortune-teller. He watched himself doing this, rather surprised: licking his fingertips, steeling himself briefly, plunging his hand into the fire before he could think about it further—and regretted the gesture almost immediately. Fat Mam Etteilla received the cards as her due, tucked them away without comment like a handkerchief in the sleeve of her grubby cotton dress. And as soon as he saw that he had

burned himself, Ashlyme felt ill and resentful. Audsley
King's behavior had caused him to act without thinking.
He marched over to her.

"It was not fair to burn the portrait," he said. "Or the
cards. We cannot make you immortal."

She stared up at him until she had forced him to look
away.

"You are only playing at this!" he shouted. "I thought
you had rejected the poses of the High City." He walked
off angrily, waving his arms. "You must make up your
mind what you really want if you want me to help you at
all."

She coughed painfully.

"I am already dead as far as the High City is concerned,"
she called after him. "Why should they have a portrait of
me? They are all up there, waiting to bid for it, like vul-
tures!"

He forced himself to ignore this, although he knew it
was probably true. He got hold of a stick and poked about
with it in the fire, trying to make out which of the tarry
flakes of ash had been his canvas, which the unfortunate
Fat Mam's cards. Slowly his anger wore off and he stopped
trembling. He blew on his smarting finger ends. When he
was able to turn round again, he found the fortune-teller
standing patiently behind him, supporting Audsley King in
her arms like a tired child. She was too weak to cause them
any further trouble. Silently they carried her inside. When
Ashlyme looked down from the first landing, the fire had
gone out and the corners of the garden had filled up with
shadows. A small wind licked the embers, so that they
blazed up briefly the color of senna flowers, silhouetting
his easel as it stood there like a small bony animal tethered
and waiting for its owner.

Halfway up the stairs, a thin line of blood ran out of the
corner of Audsley King's mouth. Her eyes widened, bright-

ened, dulled. "I have such bad dreams about fish," she said
drowsily. "Can't we go up some other way?"

What was Ashlyme to do?

"Audsley King has changed her mind," he wrote opti-
mistically in a note to his friend Buffeau, though in fact he
was far from sure of it. "I shall come and see you immediately."

Unsure of his reception—after all, he had not only abandoned the astronomer during the debacle in the Rue Serpolet,
he had ignored him thereafter—he waited nervously for a
reply; but none came. "We must make new plans," he had
written, and yet, when it came to planning he found his
brain full of contradictory considerations, or else as empty
as a new canvas. "Audsley King must have somewhere to
live, for instance. She must have money." However distasteful it was to him he should, he knew, go and see
Paulinus Rack, with whom he could arrange such things.
But the longer it took Buffeau to reply to his note, the less
faith he had in Audsley King's change of mind and the
longer he took refuge in his studio—biting his pen, listening
to the rain drip into the attic, trying to conjure up in his
mind's eye a picture of the thin, intense provincial girl who
had arrived in Viriconium twenty years ago to shock the
artistic establishment of the day with the suppressed violence
and frozen sexual somnambulism of her self-portraits.

"Hoping to find you well," he had finished. "Your old
friend Ashlyme." Was Emmet Buffeau ignoring him out of
pique? Should he go and see him anyway?

While he wasted his energy speculating thus, unaware
that he had so little time left at his disposal, autumn, like
a thin melancholy, settled itself into the plague zone. Down
there it was as if the world had become as flimsy as the
muslin curtains at an old woman's window in the Via Gellia:
as if the actual essence of the world were too old to care
anymore about keeping up appearances. With the first frosts,

unknown wasting diseases had swept the Low City; and the
quarantine police, unable to deal with the situation, unsure
even whether the new phthisias and fevers were contagious,
had panicked and begun to seal and burn the houses of the
dead. For days the dusty avenues and abandoned alleys had
been full of reluctant fires, flickering at night like blue gas
flames, as feeble and debilitated as the zone itself, which
now crept quietly over its original boundary at the pleasure
canal, inundating Lime Walk and stealing up toward the
ponderous great houses, the banks of anemones, the tall
pastel towers of the High City. Alves held out on its high
spur, eccentric and insular in a grayish sea.

As the plague tightened its grip, so the Beezley brothers
tried harder to become human.

"If indeed these brothers did create the city 'from a handful of dust,'" Ashlyme told his journal, "they seem to have
done so only in order to vandalize it. They contribute nothing. They get into the wineshops at night and steal from the
barrels. When they go fishing in the pleasure canal, it is
only to fill a jam jar full of mud and stagger home at
midnight as pissed as the newts they have been able to
discern, always out of reach, in the cloudy water." But if
the Beezley brothers felt from afar the warmth of Ashlyme's
disapproval, they did not show it. They continued to grin
and snicker nightly in the queue at Agden Fincher's pie
shop; they continued to hunt rats with cudgels and small
dogs among the derelict suburbs of the plague zone, taking
huge hauls of these vermin from the boarded-up warehouses
and empty cellars and trying to sell them for a shilling a
time to astonished restauranteurs on the Margarethestrasse.
"Their imagination," complained Ashlyme, "is vile and
wayward." And as if in response to this, they invented
donkey jackets, wellington boots, and small white plastic
trays covered in congealed food with which they littered the
gutters of Mynned.

The High City followed these adventures with an indul-

gent eye: "Besotted," as Ashlyme expressed it one day to
the Marchioness "L," "by a vitality it admires but dare not
emulate."

The Marchioness gave him a vague, propitiatory smile.

"I'm sure we none of us begrudge them their youth,"
she said. "And they do take our minds wonderfully off our
present troubles!" She leaned forward. "Master Ashlyme, I
fear that Paulinus Rack will have to abandon *Die Traumunden Knaben.*" She waved her hand in the general direction of the Low City. "In the present situation we all feel
very strongly that we should have something less gloomy
in the theater. Of course, it is a pity that we shall not now
see Audsley King's marvelous stage sets...." Here she left
an expectant pause and, when Ashlyme failed to respond,
reminded him gently, "Master Ashlyme, we do so rely on
you for our news of Audsley King...."

"Audsley King is near to death," he answered. "Every
time I go there she has allowed herself closer to the brink."
He paced agitatedly up and down the studio. "Even now I
believe she might be saved. But I will not force her to leave
that place: I find that for me to act, the decision must be
hers." He bit his lip. To his horror he found himself ad-
mitting, "Marchioness, I am in despair. Can *you* believe
she wishes to die?"

This question seemed to take the Marchioness by surprise. She stared at him thoughtfully for some time, as if
trying to assess his sincerity (or perhaps her own). Then
she said meditatively:

"Did you know that Audsley King was once married to
Paulinus Rack?"

Ashlyme looked at her in astonishment.

"It was a long time ago. You are certainly too young to
remember. The marriage ended when Rack first made his
name in the High City, with those sentimental watercolors
of life in the Artists Quarter. At the Bistro Californium they

never forgave him for 'Bohemian Days.' He had been a leading light in their 'new movement,' you see. They held a funeral, complete with ornate coffin, which they said was the 'funeral of Art in Viriconium.' Audsley King was the first to throw earth on the coffin when they buried it on Allman's Heath. Later she would claim that her husband had died of syphilis: a symbolic punishment."

The Marchioness thought for a moment. "Of course," she went on, "Rack's later behavior rather tended to confirm their opinion of him."

She got up to leave. Pulling on her gloves, she said, "You are very fond of her, Master Ashlyme. You must not allow her to bully you because of that."

She paused at Ashlyme's front door to admire the city. Sunshine and showers had filled the streets of Mynned with a slanting watercolorist's light; a bank of cloud was advancing from the west, edged at its summit with silver and tinged beneath with the soft purplish gray of pigeon feathers. "What a delightful afternoon it is!" she exclaimed. "I shall walk." But she lingered on the pavement as if trying to decide whether to add something to what she had already said. "Audsley King, you know, was a spoiled child. She has never made up her mind between public acclaim— which she sees, rightly or wrongly, as destructive of the true artistic impulse—and obscurity, which by her nature she cannot tolerate."

Ashlyme said neutrally, "She doesn't respect the judgement of the High City."

"Just so," said the Marchioness, looking out across the jumbled roofs of the Quarter. "I expect you are right." She smiled sadly. "We must hope she has more faith in yours."

When she had gone Ashlyme sat in the studio like a stone. "Married to Paulinus Rack!" he said to himself; and, "'Something less gloomy in the theatre'! Has no one told them up here that the world is coming to an end?" He got up suddenly and hurried out. The Marchioness had convinced him, as she had perhaps intended, that action was still possible.

The afternoon was slipping away into evening as he made his way up the long hill to Alves. He saw immediately that there was something wrong. A strange flat light hung round the old towers so that he seemed to be looking at them through dirty glass; the cries of the jackdaws as they wheeled round the dome of the derelict palace had a remote and uninflected note, as if they came from much further away; the peeling middle-class villas on the slopes below had aged since his last visit, and their overgrown gardens were full of household rubbish and decaying bricks. A dog trotted aimlessly about in the road ahead of him, sniffing the dust as it whirled around in cold little circles. The hill seemed endless. Halfway up it he broke into a run. He could not have explained why.

Emmet Buffeau's door was open and the damp had blown into his rooms. A stale smell came from the alcove where he did his cooking. He lay under a cheap colored blanket in a low iron bed by the washstand. He was dead. On the floor beside him were scattered the remains of two or three meals and—as if he had dropped them and never found the strength to pick them up again—a few small ground glass lenses of different colors. Beneath the blanket his body had assumed an awkward posture, twisted partly on its side: it was as though he had contracted unevenly after death, curling up like an insect. One thin arm was bent behind his head, while the other hung over the side of the bed, its long, clumsily knuckled hand touching the floor. Perhaps he had been trying to turn over. He looked old. He looked, with his intelligent, tired eyes, his worn unshaven face and big raw ears, as defenseless, honest, and undemanding as he had ever done.

On a table by the bed were some sheets of paper which he had covered with numbered notes in a spiky, erratic hand. Though the notes were unrelated, the numbers gave them a mad air of continuity, as if they were intended as steps in a logical argument. "No one has come to visit me in my illness," read one. "Hindering the scientist is a crime; it is murdering knowledge in the bud!" claimed another. "Why have I never received sufficient finance?" he asked himself, and answered: "Because I have never convinced them of the significance of the *stars,* among which mankind once flew." How long had he lain there, writing when he could, staring at the moldy shapes on the wall, when fatigue overcame him and sleep evaded him, unable to prevent himself from speculating, formulating, rationalizing? "I must always remember that Art is as important as Science, and contain my impatience!"

Poor Emmet Buffeau! The world had puzzled him by its indifference, but he blamed no one.

Strewn haphazardly round the room were the curious flannel bandages in which he had swaddled himself for the "rescue" of Audsley King. Ashlyme stared dumbly at them. In his mind's eye he saw Buffeau quite clearly: arguing with the women on the dusty staircase, pushing the empty hand-cart in erratic spurts along the Rue Serpolet in the rain, hopping from one foot to the other in the deserted observatory as he fought to free himself from the stinking confinement of the horse's-head mask. How long had he waited for Ashlyme to come and reassure him that he was safe?

The observatory was in disorder. The rooflights had been left open to admit a wet, chilly air, which had stripped from the walls the last of Buffeau's charts. Some crisis in his illness had prompted him to stagger in here and collapse among his telescopes; or perhaps he had simply destroyed them out of despair. Bent brass tubing littered the floor; and when he went over to examine it, Ashlyme felt the little

lenses crush beneath his feet like sugared anemones. He
rubbed the condensation from a pane of glass and looked
out over the Low City. He could see nothing. He could feel
nothing. Night was approaching. The ramshackle greenhouse seemed to rush through the twilight like a ship. He
had an overwhelming sense of disaster. He knew that if he
admired Audsley King, then he had loved Emmet Buffeau.

He bent to the eyepiece of one of the broken telescopes.

For a second he thought he could see a vast white plain,
arranged geometrically, on which were hundreds of stone
catafalques stretching away to a curved horizon. An im-
placable light slanted down on them, but it began to fade
before he had understood the scene before him.

He heard a sound in the other room.

When he went to see what it was, he found that a de-
tachment of the quarantine police had arrived. They filled
the place up. Black uniforms, blue-tinted spectacles, and
huge dogs on leads gave them an air of bravado and effi-
ciency. But behind the spectacles their eyes were nervous,
and after a hurried examination of Buffeau's corpse two of
them began pouring oil on the bedclothes, the woodwork,
and the walls above the bed. Two more pushed past Ashlyme
into the observatory and set about smashing windows to
create a good through-draft. The rest stood about, chuckling
over Buffeau's underwear, rifling through his papers, and
dragging the dogs off the stale food in the alcove. Despite
all this they were not unkind men, and they were surprised
to find Ashlyme in the house.

"What are you doing?" he demanded. "Who sent you
here?"

They took him quietly aside. In cases like this, they
explained, cremation was the rule: although they didn't,
personally, enjoy the work. "Your father here died three
days ago, we don't know what of," they said. They had
only just got round to him, due to pressure of work. "It's

so difficult now to get places to burn properly." Recently
an old woman in Henrietta Street had taken three attempts,
a baker's family at the lower end of the Margarethestrasse
five. All this was very time-consuming. "These rooms should
have been sealed until we arrived." They didn't know how
Ashlyme had got in. It was not that they didn't admire his
courage, but there was nothing he could do here now.

"He wasn't my father," said Ashlyme dully. "Why are
you burning him? At least his work should be saved!"

"It all has to go," they repeated patiently. They were
used to the protests of the bereaved. "We don't know what
he died of, you see. Alves is in the plague zone now. You
want to foot it while you can!"

The plague zone.

A few minutes later Ashlyme stood in the street staring
up at the top of the building. A subdued, almost reluctant
explosion shook it suddenly, and glass showered down from
the penthouse. Strange slow blue flames issued from its
upper windows, flames so pale they seemed transparent
against the great black bulk of the hill behind. "This house
was always in a plague zone," said Ashlyme miserably.
"That is why all our schemes came to nothing." All at once
he was terrified that the same thing might be happening
across the city at Audsley King's house: the thick oil, the
smashed windows, the dilatory flames. He ran off down the
hill. When he looked back the peculiar fire had already lost
its force and he could see only a knot of dark figures in the
middle of the avenue.

The High City had succumbed. In one night the plague
zone had extended its boundaries by two miles, perhaps
three. Ashlyme found himself alone in a place he hardly
recognized. Later he was to write:

"A quiet shabbiness seemed to have descended unnoticed
on the squares and avenues. Waste paper blew round my
legs as I crossed the empty perspectives of the Atteline Way;

the bowls of the everlasting foundations at Delpine Square were dry and dusty, the flagstones slippery with birdlime underfoot; insects circled and fell in the orange lamplight along the Camine Auriale. The plague had penetrated everywhere. All evening the salons and drawing rooms of the High City had been haunted by silences, pauses, faux pas: if anyone heard me when I flung myself exhausted against some well-known front door to get my breath, it was only as another intrusion, a harsh and lonely sound which relieved briefly the stultified conversation, the unending dinner with its lukewarm sauces and overcooked mutton, or the curiously flat tone of the visiting violinist (who subsequently shook his instrument and complained, 'I find the ambience rather *unsympathetic* tonight.')

"This psychological disorder of the city was reflected in a new disorder of its streets. It was the city I knew, and yet I could not find my way about it. Avenue turned into endless avenue. Alleys turned back on themselves. The familiar roads repeated themselves infinitely in rows of dusty chestnut trees and iron railings. If I found my way in the gardens of the Haadenbosk, I lost it again on the Pont des Arts, and ended up looking down at my own reflection dissolving in the oily water. As I ran, the grief and shame I had felt over my friend's death struggled with a rapidly growing fear for the safety of Audsley King. In this way I came eventually—by luck or destiny—to the top of the Gabelline Stairs."

Here he encountered the Beezley brothers, Gog and Matey, who came reeling up from the Low City toward him with their arms full of empty bottles. They had been spitting on the floor all night at Agden Fincher's pie shop. As soon as they saw Ashlyme bearing down on them, they gave him queasy grins and reeled off the way they had come, pushing and shoving one another guiltily and whispering, "Blimey, it's the vicar!" But at the bottom of the stairs, near that small iron gate through which Ashlyme would have to pass if he wanted to enter the Low City, they seemed to falter suddenly. They stood in his way, sniffing and hawking and wiping their noses on the backs of their hands.

"Let me through that gate!" panted Ashlyme. "Do you think I want to waste my time with you? Because of you one of my friends is already dead!"

They stared, embarrassed, at the floor.

"Look here, Yer Honour," said Matey, "we didn't know it was Sunday. Sorry."

As he spoke he furtively used the sole of one turned-down wellington boot to scrape the fetid clay off the uppers of the other. His brother tried to tidy him up—tugging at his neckerchief, brushing vainly at the mud, fish-slime and rat-blood congealing on his jacket. A horrible smell came up from him. He looked bashfully away and began to hum:

> "Ousted out of Butlin's, Bilston & Mexborough,
> Those bold Beezley brothers,
> Lords of the Left-Hand Thread."

"Are you mad?" demanded Ashlyme.

"We've had no supper," said Gog. He spat on his hand and plastered down his brother's reeking hair.

Ashlyme thought of Emmet Buffeau, who all his life had achieved nothing but ridicule, and who now lay quiet and unshaven, surrounded by pale flames, in the iron bed up at Alves. He thought of Audsley King coughing up blood in the overcast light of the deserted studio above the Rue Serpolet. He thought of Paulinus Rack's greed, the meaningless lives of Livio Fognet and Angina Desformes, the frustrated intelligence of the Marchioness "L," which had trickled away into scandal and "art." "If you are indeed the gods of this place," he said, "you have done it nothing but harm." He made a gesture which encompassed the whole city. "Don't you see?" he appealed. "When you came down from the sky you failed us all. I have lost count of the times when you have been dragged spewing and helpless from the pleasure canal! It is not the behavior of gods or princes. And while you occupy yourselves thus you condemn us all to waste and mediocrity, madness and disorder, misery and an early death!" He stared into their big sheepish blue eyes. "Is this what you want? If you do, you have become worthless and we are better off without you!"

To begin with the Beezley brothers made a great show of paying attention to this speech. A nod was as good as a wink to them, implied the one; while by means of agitated grimaces, groans, and shrugs the other tried to convey that he too knew when things had got out of hand. Easily bored, though, they were soon trying to put Ashlyme off—imitating his facial expressions, spluttering and snickering at an unfortunate choice of phrase, pushing one another furtively when they thought he wasn't looking. In the end, even as he was urging them, "Go back to your proper places in the sky before it is too late!" they eyed each other slyly and let fall a resounding succession of belches and farts.

"Gor!" cried Matey. "What a roaster!"

"Hang on! Hang on!" warned his brother. "Here comes another one!"

A foul smell drifted up the Gabelline Stairs.

Ashlyme bit his lip. Suddenly there welled up in him all the misery he had felt since his failure to rescue Audsley King. With an incoherent shout he flung himself on his tormentors, clutching at their coats and punching out blindly. Overcome with farts and helpless laughter, they staggered back away from him. He heard himself sobbing with frustration. "You filthy stupid boys!" he wept. He plucked at their arms and tried to twist his fingers in their stubbly hair; he kicked their shins, which only made them laugh more loudly. He didn't know how to hurt them. Then he remembered the little knife he always kept for sharpening pencils. Panting and shaking, he tugged it from his pocket and held it out in front of him.

At this a curious change came over the Beezley brothers. Their cruel laughter died. They regarded Ashlyme in horror and amazement. Then, blubbering with a fear quite out of proportion to their plight, they began to run aimlessly this way and that, waving their arms in a placatory and disorganized fashion. Penned into that cramped space which is neither High City nor Low, they made no attempt to escape up the staircase but only jostled one another desperately as Ashlyme chased them round and round, the flawed blade of his knife glinting in the light from above. "Come on, Vicar!" they urged him. "Play the white man!" They blundered into the walls; they crashed into the gate and shook it wildly, but it wouldn't budge. Round and round they went. Their great red faces dripped with sweat, their eyes were wide, and small panicky sounds came out of their sagging, open mouths. And for some reason he was never able to explain, this display of weakness only offended Ashlyme further, so that he pursued them with a renewed vigor, a kind of disgusted excitement, round in circles until he was as confused and dizzy as they were.

Matey Beezley, tottering about in the gloom, bumped into his brother, jumped away with a yelp of surprise, and ran straight onto the little knife.

"Ooh," he said. "That hurt."

He looked down at himself. A quick, artless smile of disbelief crossed his great big fat face, which then collapsed like an empty bag; and he started to sob gently, as if he had glimpsed in that instant the implications of his condition. He sank to his knees, his eyes fixed on Ashlyme in perplexity and awe; he took Ashlyme's bloody hand and cradled it tenderly between his own; a shiver passed through him, and he farted suddenly into the total apprehensive silence of the Gabelline Stairs. "Make us a pie, Fincher!" he whispered. Then he fell onto his face and was still.

Fixed in an instant of violent expectancy, Ashlyme had no clear idea of what he had done. He would force things to a conclusion. "Quick!" he demanded of the remaining brother. "You must now accept the responsibilities of your state!" His grip on the knife became so urgent that cramps and spasms shook his upper body. "Tell me why you brought us all to this! Or shall I kill you too?"

Gog Beezley drew himself up with sudden dignity.

"If you had only asked yourselves what was the matter with the city," he said, "all would have been well. Audsley King would have been healed. Art would have been made whole. The energy of the Low City would have been released and the High City freed from the thrall of its mediocrity."

He hiccuped mournfully. "Now my brother lies dead upon this stair, and you must heal yourselves." He bent down and began raking through the bottles he had dropped earlier.

Ashlyme was disgusted, but could find nothing adequate to say. "Will she die, then, despite everything?" he whispered to himself. And then, in a feeble attempt to rekindle his authority, "You have not said enough!" Gog Beezley received this remark with a look of contempt. "Besides," said Ashlyme, cowed, "I did not mean to kill him."

"He was me brother!" cried Gog. "He was me only brother!"

All intelligence deserted him. He tore his hair. He stamped his feet. He let his huge mouth gape open. He raged about in front of the iron gate, picking up bottles and smashing them against the walls where in happier times he and his brother had carved their initials. Grinding his clumsy fists into his eyes, he roared and wept and howled his grief. And as his tears rolled down they seemed to dissolve the flesh of his cheeks, so that his tormented face shifted and changed before Ashlyme's astonished eyes.

His shapeless nose was washed away, his cheekbones melted and flowed away, as did his raw red ears and the pimples on his stubbly chin—his chin itself melted away like a piece of waterlogged soap. Faster and faster the tears welled up over his chapped knuckles, until they were a rivulet—a torrent—a waterfall which splashed down his barrel chest, cascaded over his feet and rushed off into an unimaginable outer darkness, cleansing the god in him of the reek of dead fish and stale wine, of all the filth he had accumulated during his sojourn in the city. So much water was needed to achieve this that it rose round Ashlyme's ankles in a black stream, full of dangerous eddies and bearing a burden of small objects washed from the god's pockets. Ashlyme bent down and dropped his knife into this stream. A gentle pressure in his skull reminded him to dabble his bloody hand until it was clean. At last everything earthly was washed away or else irretrievably changed. Gog Beezley's filthy coat and boots were washed away on the flood, and when all was done, it could be seen that he had renewed himself completely.

He was taller; his limbs, as pliable as wax under the force of his own tears, had lengthened and taken on more noble proportions. His hair had grown until it fell about his shoulders like a true god's, framing a face which had become slender, hawk-nosed and finely wrought, a face full of power and humility, blessed with remote, compassionate, and faintly amused eyes. . . .

But long before this transfiguration had completed itself, Ashlyme had shrugged and turned his back on it. What had the suffering of a god to do with him? He waded the little stream, which was gurgling into the Low City, and went out through the iron gate into the Artists Quarter. When he looked back he could see nothing but darkness on the Gabelline Stairs, and above that only the cold flickering blue flames, as if the whole of Mynned had now been set on fire by the plague police in some grand final act of despair.

A little later he saw that his shoes were quite dry. With a groan he remembered Audsley King.

He began to run.

The hour before dawn found him in the studio above the Rue Serpolet.

A cold air spilled into it as he pushed back the curtain at the end of the little passage. He saw immediately that it had not changed. There was the *fauteuil,* with its disordered green chenille cover and piles of brocade cushions. There were the windowsill pots full of geraniums in hard brown earth or small bunches of cut anemones and sol d'or. There were the silent easels, some draped, the used and unused canvases stacked against the wall, the bare gray floorboards which gave off into the still, enervated air a faint odor of dust, turpentine, geraniums, old flower-water.

In the center of all this, Fat Mam Etteilla sat on the floor with her skirts pulled up. Spread out in front of her tentatively were the five tarot cards Ashlyme had pulled from the fire in the walled garden. Cradled between the Fat Mam's thighs like a sick child, and also facing the cards, sat Audsley King. The fortune-teller's arms were wrapped round her hollow chest to comfort her; the fortune-teller's head, with its thinning hair and brass earrings, rested on her shoulder as if they had just that minute stopped whispering to one another. Audsley King, bundled up in her old fur coat in some impossible attempt to prevent her substance from evaporating off into the void which had always surrounded her, was staring down at the cards with a sly, amused expression; and there was blood caked in the corner of her smile.

"I was free!" he recalled her saying once of her arrival in the Artists Quarter from the provinces. "I was <u>free</u> at last to paint, paint, paint!"—And now painting had finally exhausted her.

She had worked desperately in those last few days, filling canvas after canvas. Most of them were simple, almost sentimental, remembered views: golden dreamy color put down thickly with a pallet knife as—in a kind of fervid tranquility, an astonishing balancing-act of desperation and calm—she sought to recapture a level of her personality she had lost or abandoned long ago. Or had she only wanted a refuge from the empty, stretched-out nights of the plague zone? The fortune-teller's cards had failed her, it was plain. In opening this other door, onto the idealized landscapes of her youth, had she committed after all that act of escapism she had always so despised? Ashlyme could not be sure.

Honey-colored stone, oak and ivy, willows and streams. Such a light poured out of them, paling the yellow lamps, overpowering the first gray suggestions of the coming dawn! A narrow road wound nowhere, choked with last year's leaves, banked with brambles and the overgrown boles of trees. Nostalgia burned out of the flat midland vistas like a pain. And she had peopled them not with the tense, repressed, violently static figures of the self-portraits and "fantasies," but with laborers and farm-people, into whose classic postures she had injected a haunted repose.

"Everything is new to me," she had scrawled hastily above them, in charcoal on torn cartridge paper. "New or unrecognizable. What a pity I should die now." And: "To die is as if one's eyes had been put out. One is abandoned by all. They have slammed the door and gone."

Ashlyme read this message aloud to himself. He blinked. He passed in front of the women and looked down at the cards.

"What do you see?" he asked the Fat Mam, for he could see nothing. But her exhausted blue eyes followed him without recognition, like the eyes of a china figure in her slack face. Suddenly there issued from her mouth a low, appalling noise in which he could distinguish no words; and she began to rock the dead painter to and fro, to and fro. She was remembering the futile, obstinate rise and fall of some lament heard in the caravansary of her youth, when as a little girl she had learned to coax out the life and enlightenment secreted in a pack of grubby cards. The corpse of Audsley King seemed to be nodding in time to the song, reawakening for an instant, so that a parody of her old energy filled the thin white face, made voracious again the lines about the mouth, and animated the long hands which had been so full of power.

He could not watch the old woman's grief. He went to the window. When he looked out, it was almost dawn and he saw the two huge brothers hanging in the sky above the Artists Quarter, resplendent in their horned and lobed scarlet armor. Mounted on vast white horses, they moved through the dark air like a new constellation, looking down in a remote but interested fashion. Beneath them the city was awakening from its long, gray, debilitating dream.

STRANGE GREAT SINS

"THIS MITE'S SINS are nothing to some I've had to swallow," boasted the sin-eater. He was a dark, energetic man of middle height and years, always nodding his head, rubbing his hands, or shifting his weight from one foot to the other, anxious to put the family at their ease. "They'll taste of vanilla and honey compared to some."

No one answered him, and he seemed to accept this readily enough—he had, after all, been privy in his life to a great deal of grief. He looked out of the window. The tide was ebbing, and the air was full of fog which had blown in from the sea. All along Henrietta Street, out of courtesy to the bereaved family, the doors and windows were open, the mirrors covered, and the fires extinguished. Frost and fog, and the smell of the distant shore: not much to occupy him. The sin-eater breathed into his cupped hands, coughed suddenly, yawned.

"I like a wind that blows off the land myself," he said.

He went and looked down at the little girl. They had laid her out two hours ago, on a bed with a spotless blue and white cover, and placed on her narrow chest a dish of salt. Gently he tapped with an outstretched finger the rim of this dish, tilting his head to hear the clear small ringing noise which was produced.

"I've been in places where they make linen garlands," he said, "and decorate them with white paper roses. Then they hang white gloves from them, one glove for each year of the kiddy's age, and keep them in the church until they fall to pieces." He nodded his head. "That's how I think of children's sins," he said. "White gloves hanging in a church."

Imagining instead perhaps the narrow cemetery behind the dunes, entered through its curious gateway formed of two huge curved whalebones, imagining perhaps the sea-holly, the gulls, and the blowing sand which covers everything, the girl's mother began to cry. The rest of the family stared helplessly at her. There was another, idiot, daughter who kicked her heels at the table and threw the scissors into the empty grate. The father, an oldish man who delivered mackerel in a cart along the Fish Road to Eame, Child's Ercall, and sometimes as far as Sour Bridge, said dully: "She were running about yesterday as happy as you please. She were always running, happy as you please." He had repeated this every half hour or so since the sin-eater's arrival, shaking his head as if in his simple pleasure at her happiness he had somehow missed a vital clue which would have enabled him to prevent her death (or at least comprehend it). His wife touched his sleeve, rubbing her eyes and trying to smile.

It was a long vigil, as they always are. Toward morning the sin-eater heard a sound of muffled revelry in the street outside: stifled laughter, the rattle of a tambourine quickly stilled, the scrape of clogs on the damp cobbles. When he looked out he could see several dim figures moving backward and forward in the sea-fog. He blinked. He narrowed his eyes and cleaned the window pane with the flat of his hand. Behind him he heard the child's father get to his feet with a deep sigh. Turning back into the room, he said, "They've brought the horse over from Shifnal, I think. Unless you've got one in the village."

The old man stared at him, at first without seeming to understand, then with growing anger; while outside they began to sing:

> "Mari Lwyd
> Horse of frost and fire
> Horse which is not a horse
> Look kindly on our celebration."

The pallid skull of the Mari could now be seen, bobbing up and down on its pole, clacking its lower jaw energetically as the wind opened the fog up into streaming ribbons and tatters, then closed it again, white and seamless like a sheet.

"Let us in and give us some beer," called a muffled but derisive voice. The idiot daughter gave a smile of delight and stared round the room as if she had heard a cupboard or a table speak; she tilted her head and whispered. There was a clatter of hooves or clogs, or perhaps it was simply the clapping of hands. The Mari's followers were dressed in rags. They danced in the fog and frost, their breath itself a fog. The masks they wore were meant to represent the long strange lugubrious head of the wasteland locust, that enormous insect which lives in the blowing sand and clinging mud of the Great Brown Desert.

"I'll give you more than beer!" shouted the old man, his face congested with his powerful frustration and grief. "I'll give you something you won't like!" He pulled the sleeves of his shirt up above his elbows; and before his wife could stop him he had rushed out among the Mari-boys, kicking and punching. They evaded him with deft hops and skips, and ran away laughing into the mist; the idiot daughter

murmured and bit her nails; the door banged emptily back
and forth in the wind. The old man had to come back into
the house, shamefaced and defeated.

"Leave them be," said his wife. "They're not worth it,
that lot from up at Shifnal."

Distantly the voices still sang:

> "Mari Lwyd
> Falls between the day and the hour
> Horse which is not a horse
> Look kindly on our feast."

The sin-eater made himself comfortable by the window
again. He scratched his head. Something in the foggy street
had stirred his memory. "The horse which is not a horse,"
he whispered dreamily.

He smiled.

"Oh, no," he said to the old man and his wife, "your
little girl's sins will be like the colored butterflies—compared to some I've tasted." And then again: "The horse
which is not a horse. I never hear those words without a
shudder. Have you ever been to Viriconium? Packed your
belongings aboard some barge at the ruined wharves of the
Yser Canal? Watched two clouds close a slot of blue in the
winter sky, so that you felt as if something had been taken
from you forever?"

Seeing that he had puzzled them, he laughed.

"I suppose not. Still . . . The horse which is not a horse . . ."

To recall the momentous events of your life (he went
on) is to pull up nettles with the flowers. When I think of
my uncle Prinsep I remember my mother first, and only
then his watery blue eyes. When I think of him I can see
the high brick walls of the lunatic asylum at Wergs, and

hear the echoing shouts from the abandoned almshouses round the Aqualate Pond.

I was not born in this trade. When I was a boy we lived in the broad plowlands around Sour Bridge. We were well enough off at my father's death to have moved to the city, but my mother was content where she was. I suppose she relied on the society she knew, and on her brothers, who were numerous and for the most part lived close. I can see her now, giving tea to these red-faced yeomen in their gaiters and rusty coats who filled our drawing room like their own placid great farm horses, bringing with them whatever the season the whole feel of a November dawn—mist in the cut-and-laid hedges, rooks cawing from the tall elms, a huge sun rising behind the bare wet lace of hawthorn. She was a woman like a china ornament, always wary of their feet.

Uncle Prinsep was her stepbrother, a very silent man who came to us for long visits without ever speaking. Many years before, after a quarrel with his own mother, he had let the family down and gone to live in Viriconium. I can see now how much my mother must have disapproved of his dress and manner (he wore a pale blue velvet suit and yellow shoes, much out of date in the city, I suspect, but always a source of amazement to us); but despite this, and although she often pretended to despise the Prinsep clan as a whole, she was unfailingly kind to him. There he sat, at the tea table, a man with a weak mouth and large skull upholstered with fat, who gave the impression of being constantly in a dream. He was filled, his silence informed us, with a melancholy beyond communication, or even comprehension, which sometimes stood in the corner of his eye like a tear. You could hear him sighing on the stairs in the morning after his bath. He patted himself dry with a soft towel.

The other uncles disliked him; my sisters regarded him

with contempt, claiming that when they were younger he
had tried to put his hands up the back of their pinafores;
but to me he was a continual delight because he was so
often used as an example of what I would become if I didn't
pay attention, and because he had once given me a book
which began:

"I was in Viriconium once. I was a much younger woman
then. What a place that is for lovers! The Locust Winter
carpets its streets with broken insects; at the corners they
sweep them into strange-smelling drifts which glow for the
space of a morning like heaps of gold before they fade
away...."

Imagine the glee with which I discovered that Uncle
Prinsep had written this himself! I could not wait to fail my
mother and go there.

One afternoon a little after the spring thaw, when I was
eighteen or nineteen, he arrived unexpectedly and stood on
the doorstep, shaking his coat under a sky the color of zinc.
He seemed distracted; but at the tea table his tongue was
loosened at last. He talked about his journey, the weather,
his rooms in the city, which he said were untenable through
burst pipes and drafts: my mother couldn't stop him talking.
If there was a silence he would suddenly say, "I was in
mourning for six people last May," causing us to look at
our plates in embarrassment; or, "Do you think that souls
fly around and choose bodies to be born into?" My sisters
covered their mouths and spluttered, but I was mortified.

He couldn't hear enough, he said, about the family, and
he interrogated my mother—who had by now begun to look
down at her own plate in some confusion—mercilessly
about each of the other uncles in turn. Did Dando Seferis
still go fishing when he had the chance? How was—he
snapped his fingers, he had forgotten her name—*Pernel*,
his wife? How old would the daughter be this year? When
he could pursue this no further he looked round and sighed

happily. "What wonderful cake this is!" he exclaimed; and, on being informed that it was a quite ordinary *Kuchen:* "I can't think why I've never eaten it before. Did we always have it? How nice it is to be home!" He nudged me, to my horror, and said, "You don't get cake like this in Viriconium, young man!"

Later he played the piano and sang.

He made my sisters dance with him, but only the old country dances. To see this great fat man, face shining with perspiration, shamble like a bear to the strains of "The Earl of Rone" or "The Hunting of the Jolly Wren" moved them to even greater contempt. He told us ghost stories before we went up to bed. He managed to corner me on the stairs, after I had studiously avoided his gaze all evening, to give me a green country waistcoat with some money wrapped in tissue paper in one pocket; I sat in my room looking at it and wept with fury at his lack of understanding. After we were asleep he kept my mother up, talking about their father and his political ambitions, until the small hours.

We had him for two days, during which my mother watched him anxiously. Was he drunk? Was he ill? She could not decide. Whatever it was, he went back to Viriconium on the morning of the third day, and died there a week later. In keeping with her evasive yet practical nature she told us nothing about the circumstances. "It happened in someone's house," she said with a movement of her shoulders which we recognized as both protective and censorious; and she would admit nothing more.

He was brought home to be buried. The funeral was as miserable as most winter occasions. Rain fell at intervals from a low, grayish-white sky to bedraggle the artificial flowers on the cortege and the black plumes of the funeral horses. Some of the other uncles came and stood with their hats off by the grave while rooks wheeled and cawed overhead in the rain as if they were part of the ceremony. The cemetery was frozen hard in places, already thawing in others; and the flat meadows beyond were under a single shining sheet of water, up out of which stuck a few black hedges and trees. My sisters wept because their dresses were soaked, and after all they had not meant to be horrible to anyone; my mother was quite white, and leaned heavily on my arm. I wore with defiance a pair of yellow shoes.

"Poor Prinsep!" said my mother, hugging us all on the way home. "He deserves your prayers." But it wasn't until much later that I learned the sad facts of his death, or the sadder ones of his life.

By then I could be found in the pavement cafés of Sour Bridge, with a set of my own. We favored the Red Hart Estaminet, not just for its cheap suppers and boldly colored "art posters" but because it was the haunt of visiting painters, writers, and music-hall artistes who had come from Viriconium to take the *Wasserkur* in sheds outside the town. When they weren't being hosed down with ice-cold water for their bowel disorders and gonorrheas, I suppose, it amused them to make fun of our scrubbed young faces, provincial romances, and ill-fitting suits.

It was at the Red Hart that I first met Madame de Maupassant, the famous contralto, by then a creature bent and diminished by some disease of the throat, with a voice so ravaged it was painful and frightening at the same moment to hear her speak. I could not imagine her on the stage—I didn't know then that to maintain her popularity in the city she still sang with deadly effort every night at the Prospekt Theater. I thought of her as a menacing but rather vapid old woman obsessed with certain colors, who would lean over the table and say confidentially, "When I was in church as a girl, I observed that flies would not pass through the lilac rays from a stained glass window. Again, it would appear that all internal parasites die if exposed to the various shades of lavender; the doctor is disposed to try a similar remedy in my case." Or: "An honest man will admit that his most thrilling dreams are accompanied by a violet haze. . . . Do you know the dreams I mean?"

I did.

One day she said, to my surprise, "So you're Baladine Prinsep's nephew. I knew him quite well, but he never spoke of a family. Don't you follow in his footsteps: all those years at a woman's feet, and never more than a smile! There's a patient man for you."

And she gave her characteristic croak of a laugh.

"I don't understand," I said. "What woman?"

Which made Madame de Maupassant laugh all the more. Eventually, I suppose, I persuaded her to tell me what my mother had kept from us, what Viriconium had always known.

"When your uncle came to the city," she said, "twenty years ago, he found the dancer Vera Ghillera at the height of her success, appearing twice-nightly at the Prospekt in a ballet called *The Little Hump-Backed Horse*, choreographed for her by Chevigne.

"After every performance she held court in a dressing room done out with reds and golds like a stick of sealing wax. There was a tiger-skin rug on the floor. You never saw such dim yellow lamps, brass trays, and three-legged tables decorated with every vulgar little onyx box you could mention! Here they all came to invite her to supper, and she made them sit on the tiger skin and talk about art or politics instead: Paulinus Rack the impressario, ailing and thin now, like a white ghost; Caranthides whose poems had been printed that year for the first time in a volume called *Yellow Clouds* and whose success was hardly less spectacular than her own; even Ashlyme the portrait painter came, stared at her face with a kind of irritable wonder, and went away again—his marriage to Audsley King put an end to anything like that before it could begin.

"Your uncle knew nothing about the ballet then. He saw the ballerina by chance one day as he was looking out of his window into the street.

"He was young and lonely. He had taken rooms near the asylum at Wergs, where she went in secret once a month, wrapped in a dove-gray cloak. He soon became her most ardent admirer, waiting on the stairs outside the dressing-room door, fourteen white lilies under his arm in green tissue paper. Eventually she received him, and allotted him a favored seat on one of the gilt paws of the tiger. He could be seen any night after that (though what he did in the day remained a mystery), staring up at her with a melancholy expression, taking no part in the conversation of the great men around him. She never gave him any further encouragement; she had her own affairs. Eventually he died in her presence, as uselessly as he had lived—much older then, of course."

I was profoundly shocked by this, and stung, though I tried not to show it. "Perhaps the arrangement suited him," I said bravely, trying to invest the word "arrangement" with a significance it plainly did not have. The famous contralto received this with the blank stare it deserved. "Anyway, he wrote a book about the city, *The Constant Imago*. He gave me a copy of it." I raised my voice and looked round at my friends. "It is my opinion that he was a great artist, genuinely in love with art."

Madame de Maupassant shrugged.

"I know nothing about books," she said with a sigh. "But it was your uncle's idea of conversation to sidle into a room along the wall like a servant, and when recognized say in a querulous voice, like this, 'I have never found it necessary to have such a high opinion of God. . . .' Then he would regard his audience with that watery, fishlike stare he had, having struck them dumb with incomprehension. He was the most futile man I ever knew."

I never saw her again. She soon grew tired of her cure
and went back to Viriconium, but I couldn't forget this final
judgment of my uncle. If I thought of him at all after that
it was with a kind of puzzled sympathy—I saw him walking
at night with his head bowed, along the rainy streets near
the asylum, two or three sentences of his book his only
company, with the shouts of the lunatics coming to his ears
like the cries of distant exotic animals; or looking dully out
of his window into the orange glare of the lamps, hoping
that the ballerina would pass—although he knew it was the
wrong time of the month. I remembered the provincial
waistcoat he had given me; somehow that completed my
disappointment. Then another winter closed the pavement
cafés in Sour Bridge and I forgot the author of *The Constant
Imago* until the death of my mother some years later.

My mother loved cut flowers, especially those she had
grown herself, and often kept them long after they were
withered and brown because, she said, they had given her
so much pleasure. When I think of her now she is always
in a room full of flowers, watering them from a blue and
white jug. All through her last illness she fought the nurse
over a vase of great white marguerite daisies. The nurse
said she would rather be dismissed than allow them to remain by the bed at night; it was unhealthy. My mother
promptly dismissed her. When I went into the long, quiet
room one afternoon to remonstrate with her over this, I
found her prepared.

"We must get rid of that woman," she said darkly. "She's
trying to poison me!" And then, coolly anticipating the
nurse's own arguments, "You know I can't get my breath
without a few flowers near me."

She knew she was wrong. She stared with a kind of
musing delight at the daisies, and at me. Then she sighed
suddenly.

"Your Uncle Prinsep was a silly, weak man." She clutched

my arm. "Promise me you'll have your own home, and not live like that, on the verge of someone else's life."

I promised.

"It was his mother's fault," she went on in a more practical voice. "She was a woman of powerful character. And then, you see, they lived in that huge house at the back of nowhere. She attacked the servants physically if they didn't bow to her; she had her porridge brought to her every morning from a village ten miles away, because there it was made more nearly to her taste. This behavior drove her daughters to madness and her sons out of the house, one by one. Prinsep was the youngest, and the last to go—he was painstaking in his efforts to placate her, but in the end even he found it easier not to remain."

She sighed again.

"I always had a horror that I would do the same to my own children."

Before I went to take her apologies to the nurse, she said, "You had better have this. It is the key to your Uncle Prinsep's rooms. You are old enough to live in Viriconium now; and if you must, you must." She held my wrist and put the key in the palm of my hand, a little brass thing, not very shiny. "One day when you were young," she said, "the wind broke the stems of the hollyhocks. They lay across the wall with all their beautiful flowers intact. While they could be of use like that the insects still flew in and out of them busily: I thought it a shame."

She hung on all that summer in the cool room, making our lives painful but unable to relax and let us go. During that time I often looked at the key she had given me. But I didn't use it until she died in the autumn: I was sure she wouldn't have wanted to know that I had gone to the city and turned it in its lock.

It turned easily enough after so many years, and I stood there confused for a moment on the threshold of Uncle

Prinsep's life and my own, not daring to go in. I had lost my way by the Aqualate Pond with its curious echoes and fogs; like most people who come there, I had not until then realized the extent of Viriconium, or its emptiness. But the rooms, when at last I went into them, were ordinary enough— bare gray boards with feathers of dust, a few books on the shelves, a few pictures on the whitewashed walls. In the little kitchen there was a cupboard, with some things for making tea. I was tired. There was another room, but I left it unopened and dropped my belongings on the iron bed, my boxes and cases wet with salt from passage of the Yser.

Underneath the bed with the pot for nightsoil I found two or three copies of *The Constant Imago:*

"I was in Viriconium once. I was a much younger woman then. What a place that is for lovers! The Locust Winter carpets its streets with broken insects; at the corners they sweep them into strange-smelling drifts which glow for the space of a morning like heaps of gold before they fade away...."

After I have looked in the other room, I thought, and found somewhere to put my things, I will go to sleep and perhaps wake up happier in the morning. After all I am here now. So I put the book aside and turned the key again in the lock.

When he first fell in love with Vera Ghillera, my uncle had had the walls of this room painted a dull, heavy sealing-wax red; at the window there were thick velvet curtains of the same color, pulled shut. Pictures of the ballerina were everywhere—on the walls, the tables, the mantelpiece— posing in costumes she had worn for *La Chatte, The Fire Last Wednesday at Lowth,* and *The Little Hump-Backed Horse*—painted with her little chin on her hand, looking over a railing at the sea, smiling mysteriously from under a hat. The woman herself, or her effigy made in a kind of yellow wax, lay on a catafalque in the center of the room,

her strange, compact dancer's body naked, the legs parted
in sexual invitation, the arms raised imploringly, her head
replaced by the stripped and polished brown skull of a horse.

In this room my Uncle Prinsep had hidden himself—
from me, from my mother, from Madame de Maupassant
and her set, and finally from Vera Ghillera the dancer herself, at whose feet he had sat all those years. I closed the
door and went to the window. When I pulled back the
curtains and looked out, I could see the brick walls of the
asylum, tall and finished with spikes, washed in the orange
glow of the lamplight and hear the distant, ferocious cries
of the madmen behind them.

It was dawn. The Mari-dancers were long gone, off to
Shifnal with their horse; and light was creeping down Henrietta Street like spilled milk between the cobbles. The sin-
eater coughed and cleared his throat, yawned.

His energy had left him in the night, draining his eyes
to a chalky blue color, the color of a butterfly on the cliffs
above the sea. He let his hands fall slackly in his lap and
looked at the old man, who was asleep by the hearth with
his mouth open. He looked at the surviving daughter, staring
intently at the table, then scratching patterns on it with a
spoon, tongue in the corner of her mouth. He noticed the
old man's wife—laying the new fire in the grate, filling
the kettle with water, making ready for the great meal of
fish and potatoes which would be eaten later in the day—
listening serenely to him as she went about the work, as if
this were a story, not the bitter facts of his existence.

"I left Viriconium after that," he told her, "for the deserts
in the north; and I never went back there." He moved his
shoulders suddenly, irritated perhaps because he could no
longer make these events clear enough to impress her, and
he was impatient with himself for continuing to speak. "Do

I miss it? No: nor Sour Bridge, with its dull farmers treading mud in the shuttered drawing rooms."

Frost, fog, the smell of the distant shore, dawn creeping down Henrietta Street like milk. He could hear the people raking up their fires, uncovering the mirrors and bird cages. They rubbed their hands briskly as they looked out at the morning. "If the wind changes later we shall have a fine day." At last they could shut the doors and get a bit of warmth! The little dead girl lay safely on the blue and white cover; it remained only for someone to eat the salt.

"One thing is odd, though," he said. "When I sat in my uncle's rooms and looked back over the decisions which had led me there, I saw clearly that at every turn they had been made by the dying and the dead; and I swore I would leave all that behind me."

He stared for a moment almost pleadingly at the woman.

"As you see, I have not."

She smiled: her child was safe; its soul was secure; she was content.

"That was where I first ate the salt," he said bleakly. "It lay on her breast as surely as it lies now on your dead daughter's. I don't know why my uncle put it there for me to find."

Later in the morning a wind from the land got up and blew light dashes of rain across the windows, but they were soon gone and it was a fine day. Full of potatoes and fish, tired perhaps but comfortably settled in the stomach, the sin-eater picked up his bag and swung it over his shoulder. He had taken his money and put it in his pocket. Behind him at the trestle tables in the street he could hear laughter, the clatter of plates, the beginnings of music. He breathed deeply, shrugged, made a gesture with his hands, all at once, as if to convey to himself his own sense of freedom.

He was not after all that boy from Sour Bridge, or his

Uncle Prinsep. A stocky, energetic man of middle height, he whistled off down Henrietta Street, ready to walk as far as he could. He looked inland, at the hills looming through squalls of rain. Soon he would climb up among them and let the wind blow those clean, childish little sins out of him and away.